IRISH HOLIDAY
RAVEN HILL FARM MYSTERIES
BOOK ONE

JANE E. DREW

JANE DREW PUBLISHING, LLC.

CHAPTER 1

*Q*uinn opened her eyes and squinted at the clock on her bedside table. It was almost ten. She hadn't meant to sleep so late. How many glasses of wine had she drunk last night? A dull headache told her it was too many.

Then she remembered her dream. She had been standing in an old stone house; Fiona and an old man had been there, too. In the dream, she knew the man. She was connected to him in some way. The three of them stood holding hands, agreeing to something. She had felt at peace, something she rarely felt when awake. Why did she have dreams like that? Dreams that felt so real?

Quinn sighed and then slowly pulled herself up from the bed. It was another dark, chilly day, which wasn't unusual for Chicago in December. Feeling the cold, she walked stiffly towards the bathroom. The warm shower eased her bones, and her movements became more fluid. Quinn's morning routine never varied, which made it somewhat taxing to her psyche.

Maggie, Quinn's Border terrier, sat on the bathmat as

Quinn carefully applied her makeup and then dried her short brown hair. Maggie's dark eyes, which seemed to register a look of concern, followed her every movement. Quinn smiled and reached down to pat the small dog. Maggie's tail thumped the floor in response.

Quinn looked at her reflection in the bathroom mirror. A pleasant enough face stared back at her. "What's wrong?" She asked herself out loud. As a psychologist, shouldn't she know the answer? Where had all her self-confidence gone? When had her dreams deserted her? Had they just slipped away unnoticed? She couldn't even remember what they were.

Deep down, Quinn was afraid her best years were behind her. She was forty-four. Why had she left her practice at such an early age? That had been a mistake. Hadn't she enjoyed her years as a therapist? If she were honest, she would have to admit she had just been going through the motions for the last few years. Not just in her professional life but in her personal life as well. What if it was all downhill from here? That was the thought that kept creeping into her head. Quinn sighed and swore under her breath, still unable to shake off the dream.

Maggie's whine to be let out interrupted her self-pity. Quinn turned from the mirror and gathered her clothes. Just then, the doorbell rang. She hurriedly pulled on her jeans and jumper and headed towards the front door with Maggie excitedly at her heels.

Quinn peeked through the leaded glass of the oak door. The woman on the stoop waved gaily as she caught sight of her. Quinn sighed and reluctantly opened the door. Maggie shot out into the front yard, enclosed by a well-kept white picket fence, quickly doing her business.

Fiona Fitzsimmons had been Quinn's best friend since the third grade. She now stood on the stoop with an enormous bouquet of fresh-cut flowers artfully arranged in a cheerful yellow vase. Fiona owned the small nursery, Bloomers, which specialized in exotic, hard-to-find plants. Plants were Fiona's passion, the way the mind had once been Quinn's.

"I thought these might cheer you up," Fiona said as she sat the vase on the nearest table and headed towards the kitchen.

Maggie shot back in, and Quinn closed the front door, feeling irritated that Fiona hadn't called before stopping by. Fiona was the last person she wanted to see right now.

"Fee!" said Quinn, a little exasperated.

"What?" Fiona was already halfway down the hallway.

Fiona's large purse lay open on the floor of the entryway. Maggie's head was buried deep within its interior. She snorted as she sniffed expectantly at the various objects, diligently searching for the sack of treats Fiona usually brought with her to give to the little dog.

"Oh, sorry, Mags," said Fiona with a laugh. She then reached down to pull Maggie's head out of the oversized bag; then, she rummaged through it's contents, finally producing a small bag filled with bone-shaped treats. Fiona dropped a treat into Maggie's upturned mouth and patted the small dog's head. "Here you go, girl." Maggie crunched loudly on the hard biscuit.

Fiona turned back towards the kitchen. "Anything good to eat, or do we have to go out? And by the way, I'm here to end all this melodrama. You can't just sit around this house waiting to die."

Fiona, as always, could hit the mark the way others couldn't—or at least wouldn't dare.

"What is that supposed to mean?" Quinn was indignant. "I'm not squandering my time. I have a lot on my plate. You rang the bell just as I was about to go out. I'm meeting friends for lunch."

Fiona turned to look at Quinn. "You haven't got any

friends! You've cut yourself off from everyone but me." Fiona stared at her friend, daring her to disagree.

Quinn hated the fact that Fiona saw her with such clarity. "I have not cut myself off from everyone. I'm taking a sabbatical from the outside world for a few months, that's all." Quinn sounded defensive and ridiculous, even to her ears.

"That's not true, Quinn, and you know it, but I didn't come here to argue." Fiona scanned the kitchen countertops, looking for something good to eat. She picked up a cookie jar only to find it empty. She frowned and shook her head, slightly annoyed. Then she looked at Quinn and smiled.

"Quinn, I've got an idea. I think you and I should take a trip. You've hardly been out of this house in six months, and you know that's unhealthy." Fiona emphasized the last few words, and her voice had taken on the tone she always used when what she really meant was that, as a psychologist, Quinn should know better.

"I don't know where I would find the time," replied Quinn, somewhat distractedly. "I've been meaning to get some cleaning done. This house is a mess."

Fiona stopped to stare at her friend's immaculately clean kitchen with it's spotless butcher block countertops and pristine tile flooring. Even the stainless-steel appliances bore no signs of use. Fiona laughed and shook her head.

"I think you could put that off for a week or two, Quinn."

Still not finding anything to eat, Fiona moved on to the refrigerator. She leaned in and scanned the shelves, pulling out one container of leftovers after another, popping their lids, and looking at the contents before making a disgusted face and shoving them back where they came from.

"Come on, Quinnie, we've always talked about taking a trip together, and I know just the place."

"Where?" asked Quinn, only mildly interested.

"Ireland!" Fiona excitedly slammed the refrigerator door.

Grabbing a reluctant Quinn, she then began dancing, dragging Quinn through the motions of an old-fashioned polka, something they had done as children. Quinn laughed despite herself.

Finally, Fiona let her go. Quinn thought about Fiona's grandmother and the stories she had told them about the Irish.

Fiona's paternal grandparents had both been born in Ireland. Quinn remembered Fiona's grandmother, Emma Fitzsimmons, fondly. Having no grandmother of her own, Mrs. Fitzsimmons had been an excellent substitute. She would sit Fiona and Quinn down when they were children and pour them cups of tea with copious amounts of milk and sugar. Then, she would slowly sip her own tea and, in her soft Irish accent, tell them stories of life in Ireland when she was a young girl. Both girls had been mesmerized by her stories of life on her family's small farm. It was a place where all the neighbors helped each other at harvest time, all the pigs and cows had names, and the Catholic Church was at the center of everything. Quinn knew it had always been Fiona's dream to visit Ireland. It was a place Quinn also had the desire to see.

Fiona continued more seriously, "Come on, Quinnie, Bloomers isn't that busy this time of year, and it's not like you've got anything better to do. You can't just mope around this house forever."

Fiona sighed and then began opening cabinet doors, still searching for something good to eat. Finally, she spotted a box of expensive-looking cookies. Quinn had bought them the day before at her favorite bakery.

Quinn's eyebrows shot up, "I was saving those for later!"

"To eat in front of the TV, no doubt. I'm doing you a favor by having some."

Fiona settled comfortably into one of Quinn's farm-style

kitchen chairs, slipping off her shoes and putting one leg under her before taking an enormous bite from an over-sized pecan shortbread cookie. She sat chewing content-edly, not noticing the pile of crumbs she was creating on the surface of Quinn's freshly polished pine kitchen table. Quinn had found the farmhouse-style table years ago in an antique shop and had searched for the perfect chairs to go with it. The table could easily seat twelve people, and Quinn felt a little sad that such a large table got so little use.

Quinn's kitchen was decorated in the country cottage style she loved. Green painted cabinets, butcher block coun-ters, white wood walls, and light gray stone tile floors gave the room a homey feel. South-facing windows filled the room with light, even in winter. It was her favorite room in the house, and she kept it spotless. Quinn tried not to focus on the growing pile of crumbs, as Fiona reached for a second cookie.

Fiona was a few inches taller than Quinn, with thick, chin-length ginger hair and a pale, luminous complexion. She had a pugnacious air about her, and a face that never hid her emotions. Fiona looked much younger than her years and ate like a horse, though she annoyingly never gained any weight. And she had a good heart.

Quinn sighed and pulled out a chair opposite Fiona's. Grabbing a cookie from the box, she took a bite and chewed thoughtfully. She had to admit, a trip sounded interesting. Maybe that was just what she needed. And she, again, thought of the dream.

"When would we leave? I'd have to find someone to look after Maggie, and I'd need to go shopping. I'm popping out of everything I own currently." Quinn rolled her eyes and pulled at the waist of her jeans to show Fiona how tight they were.

"I was thinking of leaving next week. That would give us enough time to get organized, don't you think?"

Fiona took another big bite of cookie and then pointed at Quinn with the remains. "Hey, what about your next-door neighbor, Mrs. Saunders? I bet she wouldn't mind watching Maggie for a few weeks. You've always said how much Maggie enjoys playing with her little dog."

Quinn thought spending a few weeks in Ireland did sound exciting. It was December, which meant there would be many other tourists, and, hopefully lots of festive decorations. Christmas was Quinn's favorite holiday. She also knew that traveling with Fiona would be fun. Oddly, they had never taken a trip together in all their years of friendship. Their lives had been so busy, though. Quinn had enjoyed a successful and busy practice as a psychologist, while Fiona had spent years building her nursery into the thriving and profitable business it now was.

Fiona had only taken on an assistant this past year, admitting she could no longer handle the workload. She had hired a young woman in her twenties named Toni Houghton. Toni was bright, likable, and hard-working, and Fiona had trained her well, so she could now feel comfortable leaving her in charge of the nursery for a few weeks.

Quinn's and Fiona's lives had been very similar in many ways. They had grown up in Somerville, a suburb of Chicago. Both came from families with alcoholic, abusive fathers and mothers who had been consumed with their own problems and had little time for theirs. Quinn's mother had treated her like an adult from an early age, expecting her to take care of herself and not be a bother. Neither Quinn nor Fiona had any siblings, and they had taken on the responsibility, as children, of caring for their parents. They solidified their friendship long ago, in the shared understanding of the painful circumstances they found themselves in. Almost from the start, they had taken care of each other, and that had never changed. Now, here they sat, feeling as though they had let the best parts of life pass them by for far too long.

Quinn finally spoke, "Okay, Fiona, let's go spend Christmas in Ireland!"

CHAPTER 2

Quinn sat, relaxing in a quaint little pub attached to a hotel in Wexford City, where she and Fiona had been staying for the past two nights. She watched from a nearby window as the lunchtime crowd hurried toward their destinations. A light drizzle—what the Irish liked to call a soft day—did nothing to dampen her spirits. The twinkling lights of the Christmas decorations added to the ambiance of the room.

Quinn loved the pubs in Ireland, and they were everywhere. Even the smallest village had one or two. The tables in the pubs usually faced outward toward the other patrons and were so small you sat elbow-to-elbow with your neighbor.

The pub, like the rest of the town, was decorated for Christmas. White lights twinkled from around the windows and there was a life size Santa in the corner of the room. The fireplace was also lit with twinkling lights and greenery.

The Irish had proven to be as friendly as the travel books had said they would be, and nowhere was that more apparent than in the pubs. People gathered there for the craic — which meant 'the talk' — and Quinn and Fiona loved spending their evenings in them, listening to the traditional Irish music, and meeting the Irish people while enjoying the Christmas ambiance.

Fiona was meeting Quinn in the pub at noon. She had wanted to get in some last-minute shopping before they moved on to another town. Fiona had already bought three woolen hats, one pair of expensive waterproof hiking boots, two sweaters (or jumpers, as the Irish called them), a jacket, and many souvenirs to take home. They had been in Ireland for only a week, but Quinn and Fiona already felt at home in this charming country. They had quickly learned to use Euros instead of dollars and had mastered driving on the 'wrong' side of the road. Quinn's new jeans were feeling roomier, thanks to all the walking they had been doing — even though she and Fiona had been feasting since their arrival on the deliciously fresh food on offer in every restaurant and pub they visited.

They had spent their first night in Ireland at the Limerick Hilton, a large, new hotel in the contemporary style that was now so much in favor. The hotel restaurant was an austere, featureless room facing a busy bridge where pedestrians and cars crossed the Shannon River. The booths were comfortable, though, and the view was inspiring, so they settled in and sat drinking Guinness and downing two bowls of the best seafood chowder either had ever tasted. They morphed into younger versions of themselves, laughing so hard they could hardly sit up straight, which, in turn, clearly annoyed the other patrons. Of course, that only made them laugh harder.

They now felt like old hands navigating their way around this small country. They had rented a small car and took turns driving, stopping where they pleased, staying in B&Bs

and small hotels.And they walked for miles daily through winding, narrow streets — through towns like Ennis, Kilkenny, and now Wexford, and sometimes out into the exquisite countryside with its mystical, often spiritual beauty.

Quinn felt remarkably at home since arriving in Ireland. But she was having dreams, the kind that always struck her as odd. She dreamed of a woman holding a copper mirror and ivory dagger. The woman seemed powerful, and Quinn felt connected to her.

Fiona finally arrived for lunch, loaded down with several large bags.

As they finished their meal, Fiona leaned back in her chair, scraping the last bits of food from her plate with her fork and placing them into her mouth.

"Don't you just love it here, Quinn? I can't believe we didn't do this sooner. My grandmother was right about this country; it is a little magical."

Quinn sighed heavily; she couldn't remember feeling this relaxed or content. "Yes, Fee, I do love it here.

Fiona unfurled a map and scrutinized it before asking, "How far to Kinsale?"

"I think it's at least a two-hour drive," said Quinn, taking a last sip of coffee. "We're getting an early enough start, though. We should be there by dinnertime. It sounds like such a lovely little harbor town. Before we get on the road, though, I want to call Mrs. Saunders to see how Maggie is doing."

After receiving a glowing report on how much fun Maggie was having playing with Mrs. Saunders' little terrier, Jake, they piled their bags—plus Fiona's purchases—into the car and set out for Kinsale.

They had been driving for over three hours when Quinn finally pulled to the side of the road and asked to see the map. Fiona indignantly passed it over and then leaned in to study it with her friend.

"I see where we missed our turn," fumed Quinn as she thumped the map with her forefinger. "Right here! We missed it when you spilled that Coke on the front seats. I told you that eating or drinking in the car is too messy."

"I can't believe you're trying to blame me for your incompetent driving," cried Fiona. "Now we'll have to find somewhere else to spend the night. We'll never make it to Kinsale before dark, and anyway, I've worn this car seat long enough for one day!"

They drove on in sullen silence for a few miles; then Quinn spotted a sign for a B&B with an arrow pointing down a narrow country road. After interpreting a 'whatever' shrug from Fiona to mean yes, Quinn turned onto the small lane and drove about a half mile before arriving at a large, well-kept white house set well back from the road. There was a long, tree-lined drive, and a brightly painted wooden sign in front that read 'Ballyfrannen Bed and Breakfast.'

They both felt their spirits lifting as they entered a lovely, large foyer with dark wooden floors, arched windows, and a sweeping staircase. Garland, with red bows and twinkling white lights, wrapped around the polished dark wood of its banister. There was a small reception desk in one corner with a bell, which Fiona rang … and then rang again.

Quinn scowled at her friend as a woman of roughly their age scurried toward them through a swinging door. Delicious aromas from a kitchen somewhere down the hall followed her like perfume.The woman wore an apron stained with what looked like jam. Her cheeks were flushed, and her hair was mussed. Her overall appearance was one of being quite round. She hurriedly scooted behind the reception desk and patted the sides of her short, curly, somewhat wiry hair before smiling at them. "Good evening to you."

"You wouldn't have two rooms available for tonight, would you?" Asked Quinn, smiling at the woman.

"We would do a' course; this time of year is usually busy, but we had two couples cancel at the last minute. I'm Margaret O'Callaghan, by the way. I live here with my parents and my older brother, Daniel. He and I, havin' never married, have both stayed on livin' at home all these years. Of course, now we're needed more than ever, as our parents are gettin' on in years. The farm takes up most of my brother's time. The B&B was my idea, so I mostly see to that. Mam helps some with the cooking, but Da can hardly get around. His arthritis is that bad."

Margaret spoke with a thick Cork accent that Quinn and Fiona found hard to understand, but they felt the warmth of her words and took comfort in the fact they had found a friendly place to spend the night.

After Margaret's brief introduction to the lounge and an invitation to use it, they were given a quick tour of the dining room, where tomorrow's breakfast would be served. Quinn and Fiona returned to the car to gather their luggage, grateful to have found such a welcoming place.

"What time would ye be havin' breakfast, then so?" Margaret asked as she led them up the stairs to two lovely and well-appointed rooms, each with an en suite bath.

"Would 9:30 be too late?" Asked Quinn as she mentally inspected the rooms. The beds looked firm and comfortable, with warm-looking quilts and beautiful mahogany headboards. There were lovely, plump, floral-patterned chairs in each room and large windows that looked out onto a pasture where a few sheep quietly grazed.

"Half-nine would be brilliant! Oh, Jesus God, I'm forgettin' supper!" With that, Margaret hurried back down the stairs.

Quinn and Fiona made up as soon as they'd settled into

their rooms. After a rejuvenating shower, Quinn found a note under her door inviting her and Fiona to join Margaret and her family for supper. Both women agreed that going out was the last thing they felt like doing, so they happily accepted the invitation.

The two friends joined the O'Callaghan's in their large, homey kitchen. Their long, narrow pine table was set with wonderful old china. Bowls and serving plates were heaped with an endless array of tasty-looking dishes.s.

Quinn and Fiona savored the delicious meal and cheerfully answered Margaret and her family's many questions. They had already experienced the Irish habit of wanting to know all there was to know about you. They were asked where in the States they were from and what they did for a living. Then, were they married, did they have any children, and were they enjoying their visit to Ireland?

Donal and Maureen O'Callaghan, Margaret's parents, who looked to be in their mid-seventies, insisted Quinn and Fiona call them by their first names. Maureen was round, like her daughter, with the same kind eyes and unruly hair; only hers was completely white. Despite her ample figure, she seemed to get around well, jumping up and down frequently during the meal to bring more food to the table. As Margaret had said, her father, Donal, was much debilitated by arthritis. The joints of his fingers were twisted and swollen. Quinn noticed the cane that leaned on the table next to him, but he was still entertaining, making Quinn and Fiona laugh with his many colorful stories. Daniel, Margaret's brother, seemed a little ill at ease and was reluctant to join in at first, but he soon warmed to the two women and proved to be a thoughtful and intelligent man. The food was fantastic. There was a pork roast with chestnut dressing, two kinds of potatoes, creamed cauliflower, stewed carrots, and a freshly baked apple pie for dessert.

After everyone was talked out, they sat around the table in quiet contentment, reluctant to end such a pleasant evening. Quinn and Fiona enjoyed the sweet, somewhat cherry aroma of the pipe Donal had lit after they had finished their pie.

"Margaret, I don't know when I've enjoyed an evening more," said Quinn. Then, looking down the table at the rest of the O'Callaghans, Quinn continued, "It has been such a pleasure to meet all of you. I wish we had more time to get to know you better."

They slowly rose from the table, still savoring the feeling of kinship. Donal, who had risen with great difficulty, followed the women into the foyer.

"It has been a great pleasure to meet ye both," said Donal. "I have a good feeling about the two of ye. I think there was a reason ye got lost and ended up here with us." His dark, intelligent eyes were full of kindness.

Quinn and Fiona were both touched by Donal's words. "Well, thank you again for such a lovely evening," said Quinn.

Quinn gave Margaret a spontaneous, brief hug, which seemed to please her. After a few more thank-you's, Quinn and Fiona bid everyone goodnight. Feeling stuffed and contented, they mounted the stairs. Neither could think of anything but sleep, so they quickly parted, each heading to her room and its big, comfortable bed.

Quinn snuggled deep into the covers, anticipating a great night's sleep. She was so glad she had agreed to this trip. It was proving to be the best experience she'd had in a long time. Feeling grateful and at peace, she quickly drifted off to sleep.

Quinn woke with a start. She had heard what sounded like laughter, or was she dreaming again? Then it came again, the same unnerving cackling from somewhere in the house. It made the hairs on the back of her neck stand on end.

Maybe she should get up and investigate, but the thought of wandering around a strange house as large as this one alone in the middle of the night only frightened her more. She was sure she had locked her bedroom door and knew Fiona would have done the same. Years of living near a big city made security second nature to both of them. Perhaps she would stay where she was and hope she had been dreaming. Feeling uneasy, she slept fitfully for the rest of the night.

Quinn woke to the sound of Fiona banging on her door. "Hurry, or we'll miss breakfast." Fiona, never one to pass up a meal, had been up for an hour and was now showered and dressed.

"You go down, and I'll be as quick as possible." Quinn wouldn't be caught dead without her hair washed and her makeup on, so it was close to thirty minutes before she appeared in the dining room. Fiona was finishing a big plate of eggs, sausages and rashers, black and white puddings, and fried mushrooms. Margaret immediately brought in another equally large plate of food for Quinn that she had kept warm in the kitchen.

"How did ye sleep?" Margaret smiled cheerfully at Quinn as she sat a small pot of tea beside her.

Quinn hesitated to mention the strange cackling she had heard, feeling it would be rude. "I slept well, Margaret."

Fiona had no such qualms. "Well, I just about came out of my bed last night. Some eerie laughing came from somewhere in the house; it kept me awake half the night. You don't keep a madwoman locked up in the attic, do you, Margaret?"

Margaret laughed good-naturedly. "That would be Pike, my brother's raven. Daniel rescued him about a year ago. It was just a wee thing back then. There was a nest under the eaves of one of our old outhouses. One night, it caught fire. Pike was lying on the ground, half dead, when my brother found him the next morning. Daniel spent weeks nursing him back to health. He keeps him in his room. He's a smart little thing, but he can sometimes make an awful racket. I don't even notice the noise anymore. I'm that used to the little bugger."

"A raven? Aren't they those big, ugly birds that will peck your eyes out?" Fiona pulled a face and then took a large bite of toast.

Daniel had just entered the dining room with a plate full of freshly baked sweet rolls. He turned toward Fiona and, with just a hint of embarrassment, said. "Ravens are scavengers who will eat just about anything. But they wouldn't be after pecking your eyes out unless ye were dead and lying in the open somewhere."

"Is that meant to be comforting?" Asked Fiona between bites.

Quinn gave Fiona a little kick under the table. Fiona scowled back at her friend.

"I would very much like to meet your raven," lied Quinn to counter Fiona's comments.

Daniel brightened at the prospect. "I'll just fetch him then. He's such a smart bird; there's no end to the tricks he can do. He comes to me when I whistle, and he can undo a latch and untie a knot faster than I can! Did ye know a raven can live as long as forty years in captivity?" Daniel was obviously quite proud of the bird.

Quinn gave Fiona a look that said, "Don't you dare say one more word." Fiona pulled another face and reached for one of the sweet rolls.

Meeting Daniel's raven, Pike, had been more intriguing than Quinn had expected. He was an enormous bird with soft, velvety-black feathers. He had strong, stout legs, which allowed him to march in a dignified way, throwing one foot in front of the other — quite unlike the aimless hopping about of most birds. His beak was large and curved and looked powerful. Daniel likened it to a Swiss Army knife. Pike's eyes were bright and intelligent, and he scrutinized you as though taking your measure. Despite herself, Quinn was quite taken with the bird.

CHAPTER 3

*A*fter breakfast, Quinn and Fiona drove into Ballyfrannen. Margaret had given them the particulars. The town center consisted of three main streets. Margaret said there was a lovely hotel called The Highgate, which was a good place for an elegant evening meal. And, of course, the town had a post office, a library, and several grocery stores, including a large Super Value. There were four excellent cafés, a health food store that sold sandwiches and scones, and seven pubs. With more than a bit of pride, Margaret added that Ballyfrannen had a cathedral with a tall spire. The cathedral was over two hundred years old and was considerably more significant than you might expect in such a small town.

After walking the three main streets and stopping at the cathedral to take pictures, Quinn and Fiona were ready for tea. They had passed the health food store on their walk, which had looked interesting. The façade was painted a bright, cheerful yellow, and a large wooden sign hung overhead that read, DAILY KNEADS. Curious, they turned back in search of it.

After settling in at a comfortable table by the window, they each ordered tea and a scone.

"If I keep eating like this, I won't be able to fit back on the plane," sighed Quinn as she spooned a little clotted cream and jam onto the scone.

"You worry too much," replied Fiona through a mouthful of scone. Large drops of jam and clotted cream fell back onto her plate.

Suddenly, the lights went out. The girl behind the counter immediately crossed herself. Quinn and Fiona looked at each other in surprise, wondering what was happening. Seeing their concern, the girl said, "When a coffin is being carried to the church, we turn the lights out in the shops as a sign of respect."

Fiona, being Catholic, immediately crossed herself, too, and Quinn, out of respect, followed suit.

They all turned to watch the little procession across the street. A group of elderly men dressed in worn suits carried a simple wooden coffin draped with a wreath of yellow and white flowers. Frail, veined hands clutched the brass handles as they slowly approached the cathedral. Their feet shuffled from the weight. Suddenly, the men stopped and bowed their heads, holding fast to the coffin. The small group of people following behind did the same. They had paused in front of a tiny shop. A faded red sign above the door read, "COUGH-LIN'S GROCERY."

The stands in front of the store held open boxes of fresh carrots, cauliflowers, cabbages, bananas, and apples. The elderly pallbearers stood in front of the small store for a long moment before resuming their slow walk toward the church.

"That was her shop," said the girl in Daily Kneads as she switched the lights back on, pointing to the little grocery store across the street. She dabbed at the corners of her eyes with the towel she was holding before adding, "Orla Dowell ran that little store for over thirty-five years, and before that, it was her father's shop. Sure, her son will be takin' it over now." She spoke the words in the soft Cork accent that Quinn and Fiona were becoming accustomed to.

Quinn sat deep in thought as Fiona and the girl chatted about other things. How wonderful to live where people knew and cared about you like that. Ballyfrannen seemed an exceptional little town, even by Irish standards. Like most towns in Ireland, Ballyfrannen's town center was lined with rows of brightly painted shopfronts, which gave way to brightly painted houses. The town was tidy and well-kept and held much activity at this time of day. People greeted each other companionably as they passed on the street. It was, all in all, a charming little village without a hint of pretense. Ballyfrannen was a place where you felt noticed — welcomed, even.

The idea forming at the back of Quinn's mind almost since arriving in Ireland had become completely obvious in the last few moments. Quinn felt the need to share her thoughts with Fiona, something she had done for almost as long as she could remember.

"Fiona, what would you say if I told you I wanted to move to Ireland and live in Ballyfrannen?" Quinn looked at her friend in a manner that made it clear she was not joking.

Fiona sat for a long moment, rubbing her bottom lip with her thumb, as she always did when deep in thought. Then, she looked at her friend of so many years.

"Quinn, I would say that you have spent your whole life doing what you felt you were supposed to do and what other people expected you to do. I would say I watched you be a good daughter to your parents, and I watched you take care of them until the day they died. I watched you put everything you had into being a good psychologist and genuinely caring about the people who came to you for help."

"Furthermore, I would say you've been a person who has always put other people's needs ahead of your own." Fiona's voice became gentler and more earnest, "I would say that, for the last few years, I have watched the light go out of your eyes and that I have been particularly worried about you since you quit your practice. I would also say that in the last week, I've watched you turn back into the person I knew when we were young. The person who always has—and always will—be my dearest friend." Fiona grabbed her friend's hand, "Quinn," Fiona started, "I would say, GO FOR IT!"

Tears sprang to Quinn's eyes as she squeezed Fiona's hand. "Oh, Fee," was all she could say, but years of kinship made more talk unnecessary.

On the ride back to O'Callaghan's B&B, Quinn and Fiona were unusually quiet. Each was lost in thought regarding their conversation at Daily Kneads. Finally, they both started to speak at once. They laughed, and then Quinn insisted that Fiona go first. Fiona hesitated for a moment and then took a deep breath.

"Quinn, would you think I was an idiot if I sold the nursery and moved to Ballyfrannen too?" Fiona stared at her friend.

Tears, again, began to well up in Quinn's eyes. "Oh, Fee, that's precisely what I'd hoped you would do!"

When they arrived at the B&B, they were both so excited and talking so fast that Margaret was afraid something terrible had happened. She hurriedly sat them down at the dining room table with yet another pot of tea and listened as they took turns explaining how this last week in Ireland had been a revelation to them. They would go home, they said, and sell most of what they owned and move to Ballyfrannen. When they finished speaking, they both turned to Margaret, awaiting a response.

Margaret sat back in her chair, round-eyed and speechless. Finally, finding her voice, she exclaimed, "Oh, Jesus God! I'll make more tea!"

Quinn and Fiona based themselves at the O'Callaghan's bed-and-breakfast while searching for the right property in Ballyfrannen. Margaret had put them in touch with a local estate agent.

Liam Madden turned out to be both knowledgeable and efficient at his job. Since they weren't sure what they were looking for, he acquainted them with the unique properties on the market. First were the townhomes, which lined the streets near the town center. The only two currently available in Ballyfrannen were minimal, with no back gardens. Quinn and Fiona discounted those, feeling they needed more space. Then there were the single-family homes, each sitting on private plots of land. There was only one of this type of property for sale in Ballyfrannen presently, and while it would have been adequate, it lacked character. Neither Quinn nor Fiona could see themselves living there. Lastly, there were five country properties near Ballyfrannen.

Quinn and Fiona were getting discouraged by their third day of viewing properties. They had considered all the town properties and four of the five country properties. None had seemed quite right. Liam wasn't sure he should even bother showing them the last property. He said it was more of a working farm since it had twenty acres. There was a small cottage currently being lived in by the owner, a cottage ruin, a barn, and several stone sheds, all needing restoration. Besides that, the old fellow who owned the property was getting senile. He had chased countless potential buyers off his land, saying they weren't the ones he was meant to sell it to.

Fiona thought they should at least look at the property. Quinn knew Fiona would probably enjoy the experience of being chased by some old farmer, but she certainly would not. She couldn't help feeling depressed and a little anxious as Liam put the car in gear and headed down yet another narrow country road.

Quinn was the first to spot the property, and her heart nearly jumped into her throat. A little stone cottage was sitting well back from the road, nestled among a stand of trees on a parcel of rolling land. It looked to Quinn like something out of a fairy tale. The cottage was south-facing with beautiful stone walls. The stone outbuildings were pleasantly clustered behind the little house. There was a stream to the west, and beyond that sat a small cottage ruin. A lovely little greenhouse sat on the east side of the property, about thirty yards from the cottage. The fact that everything was a bit dilapidated didn't affect her feelings in the least. Quinn heard Fiona's gasp of delight from the back seat and knew she had spotted the greenhouse. Quinn and Fiona jumped out of the car almost before it stopped. Liam hurried to catch up to them before they reached the front door.

Gesturing with his hands at the stone walls of the cottage, Liam said, "This whole place needs tuck-pointing, and look at the state of that roof. Don't expect too much on the inside either; Owen has done little to this place in the past thirty years."

Liam turned and knocked loudly on the front door. An old man's voice called out. "Open the door, why don't ye? I ain't gettin' any younger while ye stand out there moping about."

They entered the cottage through the unlocked front door and stood in a grim-looking sitting room. A few mismatched wooden chairs and a small wooden table furnished the room, along with a dilapidated-looking cabinet that held a few mismatched dishes. A large pot of tea sat atop the table, and a faded green plastic tablecloth was under that. The fireplace was large and of the old style, dominating one end of the room and glowing from the vast amount of peat burning within its hearth.

Owen Gilpatrick was thin and frail-looking. He perched in a worn rocking chair, near the fire, smoking a pipe and drinking tea from a large, chipped mug. There was a welcoming grin on his face. Quinn guessed him to be in his eighties.

Fiona quickly approached the old man and stuck out her hand, "Hello, Mr. Gilpatrick. I'm Fiona Fitzsimmons, and this is my friend, Quinn Langston. We've come to buy your farm."

Quinn's eyes widened as she stared at Fiona, wondering why on earth her friend would say such a thing. Then, air stirred within the room. Everything suddenly felt familiar to Quinn—even the old man.

Owen Gilpatrick beamed at Fiona before he spoke. "Well, of course, ye have — haven't I been sittin' here this long time with the kettle on waitin' for ye?"

Owen shook Fiona's outstretched hand warmly. He rose unsteadily from his chair, still holding Fiona's hand. Owen then walked Fiona to where Quinn was standing, and taking her hand, too, he looked steadily at the both of them and asked in his thick Cork accent, "What took ye so long? I'd just about given up hope, waitin' for the two of ye to get here?"

Quinn was stunned by his words, but then, she regained her composure. This felt right, and why should she question that? Quinn felt herself relax as the three of them stood, hand in hand, in front of the enormous fireplace in the sitting room of Owen Gilpatrick's cottage.

Fiona began to apologize for having taken so long to get there. Quinn felt the air stir again as a deep feeling of peace engulfed her.

Liam drew up the papers that evening, and everything was signed and settled the next day.

CHAPTER 4

Quinn and Fiona spent the rest of their time in Ireland, becoming familiar with the area around Ballyfrannen. It was a beautiful part of County Cork. The countryside was a gentle patchwork of lush green fields framed by stone fences and fuchsia hedges. Before they knew it, the time had arrived to return to the States. There was a tearful goodbye to Margaret and her family before they drove off in their rental car back toward County Clare. After one more night at the Limerick Hilton, where they sat at the same booth as before and marveled at what changed people they were from the two women who had arrived in Ireland just two weeks ago. They boarded their Aer Lingus flight and arrived in Chicago the same evening.

Once home, Quinn wasted no time. She listed her lovely old bungalow with a realtor, and just as she had hoped, it sold within the week. She sorted through her belongings, selling what she didn't want to take with her and giving a few nice pieces of furniture to Mrs. Saunders, with the rest going to The Salvation Army. Quinn was determined to fill only one large shipping container, knowing she would need far less furniture than she now owned.

Quinn walked through the rooms one last time after the movers finished packing. Memories crowded into her head as she silently bid the little house goodbye, thankful for all the years it had sheltered her. With one last look back, she turned and walked out the door.

Fiona, who lived in a small flat above her business, approached her assistant, Toni, hoping she might be interested in buying the nursery. Toni Houghton was young and eager to be in business for herself, and she knew almost as much about plants and the nursery business as Fiona. The bank was happy to give her a mortgage on the prosperous nursery. Toni would move into Fiona's old flat. Fiona was leaving all her furniture as part of the sale, and both women were more than pleased with the arrangement.

Before they knew it, Quinn and Fiona were sitting in their cottage in the Irish countryside. They spent the first few weeks in their new home cleaning and painting. Then, they bought new soft green cabinets from a local kitchen joiner and had a thick butcher block countertop installed. A Belfast kitchen sink and new "American style" appliances completed the kitchen. It all sat well with the original slate flooring.

Maggie loved tramping in and out of the cottage. She especially loved her newly acquired freedom. She could roam the entire twenty acres of the farm whenever she wanted, happily chasing rabbits, foxes, and anything else she could find. There was so little traffic on the one-lane country road that ran past the cottage that there was no danger of the little dog being hit by a car. Living in their new home near the pretty village of Ballyfrannen was everything they had hoped it would be.

Their old cottage still needed renovation, though. The

roof needed to be replaced, and the stone walls required tuck-pointing. The two bedrooms were too small, and the cramped bathroom desperately needed updating.

As usual, they asked Margaret for help. They needed to find a contractor to do the roof and the tuck-pointing and to help them design cottage additions. They wanted to add a bedroom and bath at each end of the small structure. Fiona's would be on the end nearest the greenhouse, which Fiona had already started to fill with trays of newly planted seeds. Quinn's would be on the opposite end, nearest the stream, which had the view she most admired. They would use the old bedrooms as separate studies. After years of living alone, they sometimes required a space that was all their own.

Margaret said she would send over the contractor her family had used when they added a small addition to their bed and breakfast several years ago. They had been very pleased with his work. He was a widower who had lost his wife a few years back. She was sure that Quinn and Fiona would get on well with him. His name was Colin Brodie.

QUINN HAD FORGOTTEN that this was the day she had scheduled a meeting with the contractor Margaret had recommended. She had been busy cleaning out one of the stone sheds on their property all morning. It had been full of cobwebs, dust, and rusty old pieces of long-forgotten farm tools. She couldn't wait to get out of her dirty clothes and into a hot shower. She hoped she wasn't bringing any creepy crawlies in with her. The very thought made her itch. She scratched herself vigorously as she entered the cottage through the back door. She could hear Fiona and a man's voice chatting in the sitting room. It was then that she remembered the meeting. Just as Fiona entered the kitchen to make tea, she swore under her breath.

"Wow, are you going in there looking like that?" Fiona asked. "You'll scare the poor man to death."

"What choice do I have since I can't very well strip down and shower in the kitchen sink?"

"Well, at least shake out your hair; it's full of cobwebs."

Quinn did as she was told, stepping outside and running her hands through her hair before smoothing it down and returning. I must look a mess, she thought. Oh, well, what did it matter? He was probably some pleasant old duffer who wouldn't even notice.

Quinn entered the sitting room, where Colin Brodie sat holding an iPad. He was younger than she had expected, likely only a couple of years older than her. She smiled and introduced herself, thanking him for coming. As he looked up and made eye contact, she realized what an attractive man he was, with possibly the bluest eyes she had ever seen. His hair was dark, going gray just a little at the temples. He looked muscular and fit. Thank God she had lost the weight she had gained back in the States, and she was pretty fit herself from all the work she and Fiona had been doing around the farm. But look at the way she was dressed! And for once in her life, she wasn't wearing any makeup! Quinn felt like bolting from the room, but she calmly sat in one of her slip-covered wing chairs instead.

Fiona walked in carrying a tray with tea and biscuits, looking amused. After serving the tea, Fiona began discussing the bedroom additions and the other work to be done to the cottage while Colin sat taking notes. Quinn couldn't help staring at Colin each time he looked down at his iPad. He really was the best-looking man!

Finally, Colin turned to Quinn. "Could I ask you a bit about your part of the addition now, Quinn?"

Quinn gave an embarrassed little nod. With that, Colin began asking her about room sizes, bath features, and other particulars regarding the work she wanted to be done. To her dismay, Quinn realized that she had heard nothing of what Colin and Fiona had been talking about since she had been far too busy daydreaming. A bit awkwardly, she began describing the bedroom and bath she had in mind. Suddenly, she felt embarrassed by the conversation. After all, they were discussing her bedroom, for heaven's sake.

Get a grip, Quinn thought to herself. You're acting like a teenager who has never been on a date before—not that this was a date!' Quinn had a sudden mental image of Colin Brodie holding her in his arms. Dear God, what was happening to her? Now, her tongue felt thick, and her mouth felt parched. She took a small sip of tea. What had Colin been saying just then? She felt flushed, and she wondered when he would stop asking questions and leave.

Fiona had risen to collect the dishes. After depositing them in the kitchen sink, she stood just inside the kitchen doorway, out of Colin's sight, but where Quinn could see her perfectly well. Then Fiona began to dance an Irish jig, gaily placing her hands on her hips and lifting her feet quietly but flamboyantly while giggling under her breath. Quinn felt a kind of hysterical laughter bubble up in her throat. With a great deal of effort, she forced it back down. Damn, Fiona! She always knew when Quinn was ill at ease, and she never missed an opportunity to make it worse!

What was Colin saying now? He would get back to them with an estimate by the end of the week. "Yes, that will be fine," muttered Quinn, unable to make eye contact with Colin as he stood to leave.

She tried to walk him to the door, but her feet seemed encased in oversized clown shoes. She felt like she was stepping into holes, and the door seemed miles away. Just then, Fiona came in from the kitchen and casually entered the conversation, and they both bid Colin Brodie goodbye.

Fiona practically fell down with laughter as soon as he was out the door. "You should see your face, Quinn! In all the years I've known you, I've never seen you that ill at ease!" Then Fiona noticed the thunderous look in Quinn's eyes, and, still laughing, she took off at a run for her bedroom, quickly locking the door behind her.

Quinn stood in the sitting room, feeling in total disarray. She hoped she would never have to meet Colin Brodie again, and then, suddenly, she felt sad that he was gone.

True to his word, Colin had got back to Quinn and Fiona with an estimate by the end of the week. It seemed surprisingly reasonable for the amount of work to be done, so with Quinn's approval, Fiona gave Colin the go-ahead to begin the work.

Once the work had started, Quinn tried her best to avoid Colin. She also took great pains to look her best whenever he was at their farm. She told herself it had nothing to do with him being there. She made a point of being in her bedroom or study for most of the day. She pretended to be too busy to come out and deal with any issues. Whatever it was, Fiona could handle it. She still felt like a tongue-tied schoolgirl whenever she tried to talk to him. She was sure that Colin must think she was some sort of reclusive lunatic.

One day, though, Colin caught her unaware just as she was about to leave to do some shopping in Ballyfrannen. She hadn't seen his truck drive up, but he stood at the front door when she opened it to go. "Oh, Colin, what a surprise! I was just leaving for town." To her dismay, Quinn felt herself blushing. "I think Fiona is in the greenhouse if you need to speak with her."

"It was you I wanted to speak with, if you have a minute, Dr. Langston—ahh, Quinn, I mean." Colin dropped his head and cleared his throat as he spoke, looking ill at ease.

Quinn felt an overwhelming urge to reach up and stroke

his hair. Was she going gaga? Why did she have thoughts like that when this man was around? Her feelings rose with such intensity she felt they must surely be written on her face. "I'm sorry, Colin, but I really must be leaving. I'm late as it is. Fiona will help you with whatever it is you need."

With that, Quinn was out the door and into her car before Colin could say anything else. She quickly sped down the drive. I'll be so glad when he's not around, she thought, and then she felt depressed at the prospect of not seeing him.

Colin Brodie drove away from the Gillpatrick farm, deep in thought. A strange thing had happened to him since meeting the two American women. He had fallen deeply in love. From the moment Quinn Langston walked into the sitting room that first day, everything changed for him. Being a practical man, Colin had never believed in love at first sight, feeling that was something the greeting card companies had made up—yet that was what had happened to him. He thought of Quinn, with her shiny brown hair, soft dark eyes, and lovely smile. He thought of the way she had looked at him that first day. Colin pulled his truck to the side of the road, overcome by emotion.

After losing his wife three years ago, Colin was sure he would never love a woman again. He had started dating Amy when they were both sixteen. He never had eyes for any other girl, not back then or at any other time, until the day she died. After that, a terrible emptiness had taken him over, and he was sure he would carry that emptiness to his grave. But now, here it was again, like a gift, that opening of his heart. Even though Quinn did not seem to return his feelings, he kept trying to win her over. What else could he do?

CHAPTER 5

*T*he two friends stood in the soft grass admiring their cottage. The new roof and tuck-pointing made the cottage look fresh and well-turned out. The bedroom additions merged seamlessly with the rest of the house. Colin had used stone from a nearby cottage ruin to match the existing stone of their home. It was impossible to tell where the old left off and the new began. He had done such a fantastic job with everything.

Now Fiona wanted to do some landscaping. She had been boring Quinn for weeks with the names of plants she would use. "What about a little arbor over here?" asked Fiona, pointing towards the west side of the cottage. "We could intertwine clematis with that stunning climbing rose, New Dawn. Quinn, wouldn't you love a stone path leading down to the stream? I was thinking of contacting the Irish Garden Plant Society to see if they know where I can find some Yellow Poppy seedlings, the kind developed by Richard Beamish in the early 1900s. It's called meconopsis, I think. Wouldn't it be pleasant right along here?"

Quinn couldn't care less about the names of plants, so she tuned Fiona out. She did, however, appreciate their beauty.

As Quinn and Fiona walked idly around their cottage discussing the possibilities, Daniel O'Callaghan's work truck drove up the drive. Grateful for the distraction, Quinn walked over to meet Daniel as he climbed out of the truck. "What brings you out on this fine day, Daniel?" Quinn asked.

"I have a great favor to ask of ye and Fiona," replied Daniel, looking serious and somewhat ill at ease.

"Well, we certainly owe you a great many favors after the help your family has been to us," smiled Quinn.

"It's concerning my raven, Pike." Daniel pushed the toe of his well-worn boot into the dirt, still looking ill at ease. "I've always remembered how he took to you that first day you met him. I've never seen him take to anyone like that besides me. You also seemed to like him, which brings me to why I'm here." Daniel heaved an enormous sigh as though reluctant to continue.

"As you know, Pike can make a racket sometimes, and we've been getting complaints. Margaret says Pike has to go. She says he can't be interfering with our livelihood by scaring off the guests. I know this is a lot to ask." Daniel raised his eyes and glanced in Quinn's direction before continuing. "But I can't think of another living soul I would be comfortable leaving Pike with. What I'm asking is, would you consider taking him in to live here with you?"

Quinn was taken aback by Daniel's request but also touched, knowing how much the bird meant to him. She considered before answering. "Daniel, I would have to talk to Fiona first, and I also wonder how Maggie would react."

"I think Maggie would enjoy having a playmate," laughed Fiona, who had walked over to join them.

"Playmate? What are you talking about?" responded Quinn.

"Look over there." Fiona pointed towards an open area near the stream.

Daniel and Quinn turned in unison. Pike, who had ridden with Daniel in his truck, swooped to the ground, grabbing Maggie's favorite ball before flying off a short distance. He then dropped the ball back onto the ground. Watching Pike as she ran, Maggie crossed the front garden at lightning speed to retrieve the ball. She then laid it on the ground in front of Pike. Pike grabbed it up again in his beak and flew off, and the game began again.

"I've never seen anything like that in my life," laughed Quinn. "Daniel, if it's alright with Fiona, you've found Pike a new home."

Fiona nodded in agreement before asking Daniel in for tea. Daniel ran back to his truck to fetch Pike's large cage and food, which comprised everything from high-quality dog food to peanuts, sunflower seeds, corn, fresh fruit, mealy worms, and crushed hard-boiled eggs, with the shells left on.

Over the following days, Quinn spent time on the Internet researching ravens and was a little amazed at what she found. Ravens were part of the corvid family, along with magpies and crows. They possessed one of the largest brains in the bird world. They were also blessed with a rich awareness of life, and they had a sense of humor. When flying, ravens would sometimes do loops, rolls, dives, or even fly upside down, just for fun. They also knew how to hang upside down like a bat on a tree limb and swing back and forth, which was very entertaining. Ravens could manipulate other animals and humans, as Quinn would soon learn.

Pike had joined her "flock," meaning he would eat when she ate, sleep when she slept, go with her wherever she went, and protect her if necessary. When Quinn went to town or ran errands, Pike would fly alongside her car, always staying close and making eye contact with her occasionally. He would behave this way with other ravens in the wild, so it was natural for him to act this way with Quinn. It didn't take Quinn long to become devoted to the bird, and the bird to her. She developed a special call for him: two long, high whistles and one short, low whistle. Wherever Pike was, he would come when he heard her call. Pike was bright, clever, mischievous, and an absolute pain at times, but she couldn't imagine life without him. Quinn and Fiona even named the farm after the bird. They had a piece of stone engraved and placed by the front door with the new name. It read, "RAVEN HILL FARM."

CHAPTER 6

$\mathcal{D}$espite being happy with how life was turning out for her and Fiona, living on their little farm, Quinn moped about. It was ridiculous that she still constantly thought about Colin Brodie. She decided she needed something to occupy her time.

Quinn had noticed a small white building in the town center with the sign "Ballyfrannen Mental Health Clinic" above it. She was thinking of volunteering as a therapist a few days a week. That might be just the distraction she required. Rather excitedly, she gave them a call.

The understaffed clinic was happy to accept Quinn's offer of volunteering part-time. Cathal Fagan, the clinic's director, gave Quinn a tour of the small building and then escorted her into a compact but cheerful little room that would be hers. No one else was using it just now, so she should make it her own, Cathal had said.

A few days later, Quinn moved into her new office. She brought several pots of red geraniums and placed them on the deep windowsill to brighten the small space. Then she took stock of the room. The walls were painted a pleasant shade of blue. There was a small wooden desk with a matching chair and an old lamp, two comfortable blue plastic chairs, and a spindly little table with a large box of tissues on top. This would do fine, she thought. She was eager to get back to work.

Quinn's first patient was a nineteen-year-old girl with long blond hair, pale skin, and a bad complexion. As she entered the office and tentatively sat down, Quinn noticed a fragility about her that seemed odd for one so young. Her first impression of the girl was that she might be pretty if she didn't seem so cowed by life. Why is self-esteem so scarce in this modern world? Quinn spoke gently to the girl, trying to put her at ease as she asked her questions about her life.

She said she worked as a checker at the local Centra and enjoyed the job well enough. When asked about her family, she said her father had left when she was eight. She had recently been in contact with him again, but just as they were becoming re-acquainted, he had died in a house fire in Cork City. He had been smoking in bed and was drunk. She had one brother, who was three years younger and still in school. Her mother worked hard at a pub job to support the three of them, but with the long hours, there wasn't much time left for family life. Megan and her brother, Kyle, mainly had made do for themselves growing up. Their grandmother had helped when she could, but her health had not been the best. Megan had been close to her grandmother, who had recently passed away.

On top of everything else, Megan's boyfriend was pressuring her to get married. Megan had been having panic attacks for the last several weeks, which were getting increasingly worse. Her doctor had prescribed a Diazepam-type tranquilizer, but it had been little help in relieving her anxiety.

Themes of abandonment and loss were common enough

causes for panic attacks. The added pressure of trying to commit to marriage after watching her parents' marriage fail was undoubtedly adding to the girl's problems.

Quinn spent the hour speaking reassuringly to Megan. She planned to build the girl's self-confidence and help her through her abandonment and commitment issues. After scheduling an appointment for the following week, Megan left, looking a little less anxious than when she arrived.

Quinn sat back in her chair, feeling the satisfaction she always felt when she knew she could make a real difference in someone's life. She had missed her work and was glad for the opportunity to spend time at it again.

Her next patient was Jozef Abram, a man of about thirty-five. He had a thick build and looked used to hard physical labor. He had well-muscled arms. His whole body seemed coiled with a kind of nervous energy. He spoke with a heavy Eastern European accent that Quinn had trouble under-standing. He also looked less than happy to be sitting in her office.

"Hello, Jozef. May I call you Josef? I'm Dr. Langston. Could we start by telling me why you've come to see me?"

Jozef, unexpectedly began to sob. His large shoulders shook with the force of his emotion. "I'm here because my wife, she tells me if I don't come she will leave me. She will take my children and go back to Poland and live with her mother, the old bat! So, I have no choice; either I come here, or I lose my children and my wife." Jozef swiped at his eyes, refusing the tissue Quinn offered.

Suddenly, Jozef stopped sobbing and raised his head out of his hands. The look he gave Quinn was surly, almost threatening.

Quinn had seen this before. This man suffered from severe anger issues. This wouldn't be a quick fix; that was for sure. Quinn cleared her throat and sat up straighter in her chair, now more alert. She could see the anger glinting in his eyes as though he would like nothing better than to get up and punch her. Quinn knew he meant to scare her, to put her in her place, like he probably did his wife, to let her know who was in charge. What he had no way of knowing was how much Quinn hated bullies.

"Mr. Abram!" Quinn's voice boomed with authority. "You need to sit back in your chair and wipe that threatening look off your face, or I will be forced to call security." (There was no security in the small clinic that she knew of.) "Furthermore, if you want my help, you will treat me with respect," Quinn leaned far forward in her chair towards her patient. Again, in a booming voice, "Are we clear on that?"

All the wind went out of Jozef's sails as he, again, put his head in his hands and wept. "I'm sorry. I know I have the anger problem. My wife, she tells me I have this problem. I want to change, but how do you change such a thing? You tell me that?" He looked up at Quinn as though he expected an answer.

It was an excellent question. Most people acted as they did because they had grown up watching the people around them model that behavior. Contrary to what most popular talk shows would have you believe, people behaved the way they did, not because they wanted to, but because that was all they knew.

The rest of the session passed uneventfully, with Quinn asking Jozef about his childhood and other relevant details regarding his past.

It was late afternoon by the time Quinn arrived back at the cottage. She had enjoyed her first day of work despite Jozef Abram—or maybe even because of him. Giving him insight and better tools to manage his life would be challenging. Quinn knew his family's happiness hung in the balance. She would do her best to help them.

Quinn lay in bed that night, feeling contented. The over-sized farmhouse-style bed she had brought from the States fit comfortably in the space. Everything in her new room was comforting. The pine ceiling was painted a soft white, and the walls were a pale yellow.Wide wood planks, stained the color of honey, made up the flooring. Across from her bed, she had hung a painting of sheep grazing in a pasture, with an old-fashioned Irish cottage in the background. Quinn had found the painting in an art gallery in Cork City and bought it because it reminded her of everything she loved most about Ireland. She had hung it where she would see it every night. Quinn wanted to remember to be grateful that she and Fiona had come to Ireland and found this special cottage on this beautiful farm that now was theirs.

Quinn was also grateful to be working as a psychologist again. She had missed her profession more than she realized, and she still felt passionate about helping those who came to her for guidance.

She thought about her childhood. Her father had been an alcoholic. When he drank, he became another person, a mean, belligerent, threatening drunk who would terrorize her mother and occasionally become violent. Quinn would curl up in bed at those times, afraid to do anything else. She feared her father's anger and was terrified he would injure or kill her mother.

Quinn had spent her entire childhood trying to fix her parents. Of course, that was an impossible task for a child. Still, being a fixer became part of her identity. She would always have to try to make a difference, and it still hurt, after all these years, that she hadn't been able to do that for them.

The next day, Quinn sat in her small office waiting for the only patient she had scheduled that afternoon, a forty-year-old woman seeking treatment for weight loss. Her name was Agnes Meek.

Agnes walked into Quinn's office with a flourish and a big smile. Quinn guessed she had to weigh at least three hundred pounds. She was wearing so much perfume Quinn's eyes stung. Her brown hair was past her shoulders and streaked with blonde highlights. Quinn noticed her heavy makeup and jewelry and freshly painted nails. Her clothes were well-made, and she was carrying what looked to be a costly designer purse.

Agnes sat down and sighed rather dramatically. She unwound a sizeable purple scarf from around her neck and laid it on the back of her chair.

"I can't believe I'm here! I'm so excited at the thought of losing weight. I know you will help me and that we'll end up being the best of friends!"

Quinn thought that was quite a lot of expectations since she had not yet spoken. "Hello, Agnes, I'm Dr. Langston. Why don't we start by getting some information about why you're here?"

Agnes enlarged her eyes and blinked, turning her head slightly to the side as she did so. She seemed perplexed by Quinn's question. "I've already told you why I'm here; I'm here to lose weight."

Quinn sighed mentally. People like this could be hard to deal with. They seemed friendly enough, but they usually wanted total control. Agnes seemed to be a classic passive-aggressive personality.

"I'm sorry if I've confused you, Agnes. I meant that we must explore the reasons for your weight gain and what might keep you from losing weight."

"Nothing is bothering me if that's what you mean; my life is wonderful. I just need to lose weight, that's all. Plain and simple. Can't you hypnotize me or something?" Agnes was still smiling.

"Well, first, I'd like to get a little of your family history, if you don't mind, Agnes."

"Family history? Oh, you mean my childhood. It was fine; I had a wonderful childhood. What else do you need to know?" Agnes was still smiling.

Quinn could tell this would not be easy. She sighed and tried again. "Since your childhood was fine, could you just give me a little more detail so I have something to write down?"

"Well, like I said, it was fine. My parents were wonderful and loved me and my sister a lot—especially me. They were sad, of course, when my sister died, but they got over it, and we were happy again, and we've been happy ever since." Agnes kept smiling.

"You had a sister who died?"

"I just told you that."

"Could you tell me how she died?"

"She drowned in the stream near our house."

"How old was your sister when she died? How old were you when she died?"

"Why so many questions about my sister? She was three when she died, and I was seven. She fell into the stream near our house. We lived a few miles outside Ballyfrannen back then. I don't see what is so interesting about that. It was just one of those freak accidents that happen. I don't even think about it anymore."

Quinn paused momentarily before asking, "Agnes, were you with your sister when she died?"

"No, not exactly. I was supposed to be watching her, but I had gone off to play somewhere else. It wasn't any fun to play with my sister, so I left her by the stream that ran alongside our farm and went to play. She was too small to swing. I would push her sometimes since she couldn't do it herself, but I went off by myself to swing that time. I told you that was a long time ago, and I don't even think about it anymore. Why are you so interested in that?" Agnes's smile had lost some of its luster but was still there.

"Agnes, just one more question about your sister's death. Did your parents blame you when she died? Did they ever say anything about you leaving her?"

"Oh, sure, they said I shouldn't have left her." They said, 'What kind of big sister would go off and leave her little sister by a stream, where she could fall in and drown?' "But I knew they still loved me. They had always loved me best, anyway. I guess I shouldn't say that, but it's true."

"Agnes, are your parents still living?"

"Yes."

"And your relationship is still good?"

"Of course, its good. What kind of question is that?"

"When was the last time you saw your parents, if I might ask?"

"Well, let's see. I guess it's been about twenty years. As soon as I grew up, they moved away. They're so busy that they don't have time to come and visit, but they love me. I know they love me; they're just busy. I don't see why you are asking all these questions when I've told you. I'm just here because I can't lose any weight."

Quinn felt a knot forming in her right shoulder. Agnes sniffed and reached into her purse to retrieve a tube of lip gloss, which she then liberally applied to her pursed lips. And she was still smiling.

CHAPTER 7

*Q*uinn was excited to spend the day at the farm doing precisely what she wanted. She planned to walk out to the small orchard at the back of their land to the west. She knew that the area could do with a little tidying up. There were dead tree limbs and underbrush that needed to be dealt with. Quinn found being out on the land one of the most pleasant experiences of her new life here in Ireland. Ireland had such a quality to it, like nowhere else on earth. She didn't mind the frequent cloudy days or rain; as far as she was concerned, it was part of what made Ireland so magical.

Lost in pleasant thought, Quinn walked up a small hill and headed back towards the cottage. She had left the tree limbs and underbrush in a neat pile at the back of the property to be picked up later. As she approached the cottage, she saw a car parked in the lane she didn't recognize. Just as she entered through the back door, she heard a knock at the front door. Quinn hurried into the sitting room and opened the door to the last person she expected to see.

"Hello, Quinn. Aren't you going to invite me in?" Jack

Wyatt, Quinn's former husband, stood wearing the same smug expression Quinn knew so well. It's a shame, she thought, that once you know a person, you can never unknow them, no matter how badly you might wish to.

Quinn had met her former at the University of Illinois, where they were both majoring in psychology.

Jack was good-looking and self-assured, with dark blonde hair, blue eyes, and an easy smile. He was excellent at handling people and good at hiding his tendency towards snobbishness. Jack secretly believed that most people were inferior to him. Quinn was to discover later that this included her parents and her friends, especially Fiona — and Quinn herself. Once they were married, if anyone from her family came to visit, he was quick to get out the vacuum cleaner and cleaning supplies to remove any trace of them being in the house.

Early in their marriage, Jack made it pretty clear that Quinn didn't measure up. Once, when she had gained a couple of pounds, he had playfully grabbed her stomach and called her jelly belly. When she reacted with hurt feelings, he accused her of being too sensitive.

Quinn never got his approval or met his expectations. Life with Jack was constant criticism, which had caused Quinn to doubt herself at every turn.

Even so, for a few years, their marriage had seemed happy enough, although she would later admit she had no real standard with which to judge since her parent's marriage had been so dysfunctional. Quinn had spent her entire childhood being criticized, so Jack's treatment of her had seemed normal enough, even with all her training as a psychologist.

Once out of college, they shared a successful practice and did well financially. They could afford a large brick home in one of the most upscale neighborhoods in Summerville, and each had an expensive new luxury car. The upper-class lifestyle they lived was vital to Jack. Quinn never questioned whether it suited her as well.

One evening, about seven years into their marriage, Jack took Quinn to one of their favorite restaurants. They had enjoyed many dinners there. The place had a lovely ambiance, with its cozy booths and flickering candles that gave a lovely glow to the paneled walls and flattered the patrons. There, over a bottle of expensive wine, Jack had asked Quinn for a divorce. He said he felt they had fallen out of love with each other. When Quinn began to cry, he patted her hand and said she should be the one to move out of their home, and, as unfair as that seemed, he had also balked at the idea of her taking any of their expensive furnishings.

Because their money was tied up in their home, Quinn was forced to move into a tiny, sparsely furnished apartment with only a few thousand dollars with which to start a new life. She also had to start a new practice since Jack thought he should keep all of their old clients.

Why had she allowed her husband to take advantage of her like that—some misplaced feeling left over from child-hood that she didn't deserve better? That thought made her angry now. She had deserved better. Jack had been callous, greedy and petty towards her.

She hadn't allowed herself to be angry with him back then. She had bottled it all up and remained on good terms, telling friends that the divorce was all her fault. Her mother had taught her to protect others, not herself. Better she take the brunt of any gossip lest people think badly of Jack.

Quinn had bouts of debilitating back pain throughout those years of her life. She knew she had allowed Jack to treat her with the same disrespect her parents had, but even with all her training and knowledge, she could not seem to find the will to protect herself from such treatment. Knowing and doing were two very different things.

The one bright spot was that Quinn had turned her meager funds into a small fortune. A grateful, tech-savvy client, whom Quinn had helped overcome an incapacitating case of obsessive-compulsive disorder, had helped her navigate the stock market. She had bought stocks like Microsoft, Apple, and later, Google and Facebook before those companies were household names, making enough money to never have to worry about it again.

QUINN'S THOUGHTS of the past subsided as her back abruptly began to ache. Must be all that stooping to pick up tree limbs, she thought.

Quinn turned her attention back to Jack. Where had he come from, and why was he here?

"How long has it been since we've seen each other? Five years or more, I'll bet?" Jack seemed as cheerful and false as ever.

"Don't you want to know how I found you? Thanks, by the way, for letting me know you were moving halfway around the world."

"What are you doing here, Jack?" Quinn's voice was sharp. "And yes, I want to know how you found me."

"You're forgetting your dear neighbor, Mrs. Saunders."

There was that smug smile again. Quinn felt her stomach knot.

"You know how she adores me. She couldn't believe you had left without telling me. She was sure it was an oversight on your part and was only too happy to give me your new address, which, as I mentioned, was halfway around the world. What gives, Quinn? Have you taken leave of your senses?"

Quinn opened her mouth to give Jack an explanation for

her behavior but instead said, "Why don't you come in, Jack, and I'll fix us some tea?"

Fiona sat at the kitchen table with her reading glasses pulled halfway down her nose, browsing through the Irish Times on her laptop. As Quinn and Jack entered the room, she looked up from her reading. At the sight of Jack, her eyebrows shot up.

"Jack, what a surprise! I'm finding it hard to express my feelings at seeing you here, but they're akin to the ones I had when I was diagnosed with a severe case of food poisoning."

"Fiona!" Jack smiled. "It's good to see no one has cured you of that bad case of antisocial personality disorder you're stuck with. Although that doesn't speak highly of your professional skills, Quinn, considering all the years you two have been friends." Jack chuckled as though the exchange had been all in good fun.

Quinn and Fiona exchanged glances before Fiona said, with more than a bit of sarcasm, "Come to think of it, I'd prefer food poisoning."

"Alright, Fiona, you've conveyed your displeasure at Jack being here. Let me just go on the record and say that I didn't invite him, and I have no idea why he's here."

"Why are you here, Jack? Did you run out of people to annoy in Chicago?" Then, with a sigh of resignation, Quinn added, "Okay, we'll both stop; just tell us why you're here."

"Do I need a reason to visit my oldest and dearest friend, not to mention the only woman I have ever been married to?" There was that smug smile again.

"YES!" from Fiona.

"Alright then." Jack sighed before sitting down at the kitchen table and pouring himself a cup of tea.

Quinn and Fiona again exchanged glances.

"Things have been a little stressful in Chicago lately. People are buying self-help books and listening to podcasts instead of visiting psychologists like they used to. I'm certain that's why you retired, isn't it, Quinn? I'm sure your practice was way off from what it used to be," insisted Jack.

"No, my practice was doing just fine when I retired," replied Quinn.

"Well, things have changed since then. Psychology is not what it used to be. People expect immediate results, and when they don't get them, they stop coming. I needed a break from all that, so I came to Ireland to spend some time with you and Fiona."

"Lucky us," said Fiona, rolling her eyes.

"Fiona," warned Quinn, "we said we'd be nice."

"I never said any such thing," retorted Fiona.

"Of course, you can stay with us for a few days, Jack," said Quinn. "You can sleep in my study ... with Pike."

"Who's Pike? Not some live-in lover of Fiona's, I hope?" Jack leaned back in his chair, far too pleased with himself.

"Pike is Quinn's pet raven," said Fiona in a menacing voice. "Jack, I'd sleep with one eye open if I were you; ravens have been known to peck people's eyes out. Pike can make a terrible racket at night, too. It can make your blood run cold. We're used to it, but I wouldn't want you to have a heart attack or anything."

"Thanks for your concern, Fiona." Jack squirmed a little in his chair. "Quinn, could I just speak to you about the sleeping arrangements?"

"Relax, Jack. I'll put Pike in the sitting room while you're here."

JACK HAD BEEN their houseguest for three weeks and gave no sign of wanting to leave. His visit was turning out to be more fun than Quinn had expected. She had forgotten how charming Jack could be when he wanted. They spent their days visiting the local sites and taking long walks through the countryside. They talked a lot about the good times they'd had during their marriage, never mentioning the bad. Jack flattered Quinn with stories of how she had been the one who had built their practice and what a good therapist she was. Jack couldn't seem to do enough for her. Had he always been this considerate?

Quinn realized how wonderful it felt to be part of a couple again. They went to the movies and had frequent intimate dinners in some of Cork City's finest restaurants. Quinn had forgotten what all of that felt like. Being with Jack again reminded her of the good things that came with marriage. Fiona, of course, was avoiding Jack like the plague and making cutting remarks to Quinn about him every chance she got.

Quinn thought Jack had matured and turned into a far nicer man than the one she remembered. Maybe their divorce had been a mistake after all. She was beginning to resent Fiona's remarks, and she and Fiona had started to quarrel, which wasn't like them at all.

Jack noticed the tension between the two friends. He took every opportunity to point out Fiona's flaws whenever he and Quinn were alone together. Quinn felt it was out of concern for her welfare.

"Really, Quinn, you should think about buying out Fiona's share of the farm. I hate to see you living with someone who obviously isn't concerned about your feelings or respects your needs."

Quinn thought that didn't sound like Fiona, but she was trusting Jack's judgment more and more and her own less and less. What other motive could he have for saying such things besides her welfare? Perhaps buying the farm with Fiona had been a mistake.

Quinn was more anxious and worried than she had been

in a long time. She wasn't sleeping well and just felt "off". Equally disturbing was the fact that Quinn's back seemed to be getting worse instead of better. She really must have injured herself the day she had worked in the orchard, she thought. She seemed able to do less and less as the days wore on. Maybe she should see a chiropractor.

Jack fussed over her, which was nice. He also reminded her that she had always had problems with her back when they were married. What had she been thinking, taking on a farm at this point in her life? No wonder she was in pain. This was all too much for her, Jack said. She needed a man around the house to do the things she couldn't—someone to care for her as the years advanced.

Quinn felt Jack was making more and more sense. He had been back in her life for a month, and she was growing more and more dependent on him. Soon, she began consulting him before making any decisions at all. How had she managed so long by herself? Jack had even offered to take over her finances so she wouldn't have to bother with them. Quinn felt grateful for the help. Her life seemed to be crumbling under the weight of everything. She was vaguely aware she had felt like this before, but she couldn't think when or what had brought it on. Why was she so filled with self-doubt and incapacitated with back pain now when she was so happy to have Jack back in her life?

Her relationship with Fiona continued to deteriorate. They spent less and less time in each other's presence. What had been fun and fulfilling about their relationship such a short time ago now seemed stifling and uncomfortable. Jack continued to press Quinn about buying Fiona's share of the farm. Sadly, she felt he was right. She vowed to Jack to do it within the week.

The next evening, Jack took Quinn to one of the finest restaurants in Cork City. They sat in a cozy, quiet booth, facing each other, chatting about the past and Jack's plans for the future as they savored another candlelit dinner. The years have treated Jack well, Quinn thought as she observed him in the candlelight. She had never found him more attractive.

Jack snapped his fingers at the waiter and ordered an expensive bottle of Merlot. He smiled at Quinn as he did so, and suddenly, with horror, she saw all the falseness in that smile, all the pettiness and greed in his character, the constant infatuation with status.

A long-forgotten memory began to play at the back of Quinn's mind. Everything seemed to shift. She was beginning to feel more herself again.

"Quinn, I've been doing a lot of thinking since coming to stay with you."

Jack reached over and gently took Quinn's hand in his. He smiled, and again, Quinn realized how attractive he was, but it was a superficial attractiveness, nothing more than a mask. How had she been so taken in again by this man?

"Quinn, will you do me the honor of becoming my wife again? It would make me the happiest man in the world!"

Without waiting for an answer, Jack reached into his pocket, pulled out a large diamond ring, and placed it on Quinn's finger.

Quinn felt stunned. A sudden stabbing pain in her back made her wince and re-adjust herself in her seat. She stared at the ring for a moment. The memory that had unsettled her all evening was still trying to make its way to the surface.

Jack noticed her distraction from what he presumed would be a wonderful moment. He felt annoyed. After all, he had just said that saying yes would make him the happiest man in the world, and didn't she want to make him happy? He thought the answer was obvious.

Suddenly, the memory lurking in Quinn's subconscious

sprang full force into the forefront of her mind. "Jack, do you remember how you asked me for a divorce?"

"Vaguely, dear, but let's not dwell on unpleasant memories just now."

"Oh, let's DO!" said Quinn. "We were in a restaurant much like this one, and you had just ordered a bottle of expensive wine, much like the one we are now drinking. Then, out of the blue, you asked me for a divorce. You took my house, my furniture, and my patients, and you left me with nothing. It took me years to rebuild my life. Now I'm happier than I've ever been. I've loved living here in Ireland with Fiona on our farm, and then you show up and ruin everything!"

"And by the way, where did you get the money for such an expensive ring? You've already told me your practice is almost nonexistent. I'll bet it came from my account, didn't it?"

"Now, Quinn, you're getting far too emotional." Jack's self-assured smile had turned into a look of annoyance. "We're getting married again, so what difference does it make where the money came from to buy the ring? What's yours is mine. We can fly back to Chicago this weekend and get married, and then, once we've settled my debts, we can come back here to our farm. I'll take care of everything. I'll be the one to tell Fiona we're buying out her share, so you'll be spared the histrionics."

Jack leaned back in the booth and smiled before adding, "Quinn, you're not getting any younger. You don't want to end up old and alone, do you? This is probably the last offer of marriage you will ever get."

Quinn felt as though a fog had lifted. Why had she so easily slipped back into the old patterns from her childhood? Why had she allowed Jack to use her again? Quinn took one last sip of the expensive wine, then she stood and threw the rest in Jack's face! She could hear him sputtering as she marched out of the restaurant. God, that felt good, she thought!

Quinn pounded on the steering wheel, both from frustration and glee at finally coming to her senses! What if she had said yes? What if she had again married that obnoxious, self-serving man? In the time it took Quinn to drive home, her back had stopped hurting. Once home, Quinn wasted no time. She sat Fiona down and apologized for her behavior over the last month.

"Oh, Fee, I'm so sorry! It was so stupid of me to let Jack back into my life. I hate the way I've been treating you. It's my fault we've had so many fights. I hope you can forgive me."

Quinn had never been more aware of how much her friendship with Fiona meant to her. Now she stared at the floor as tears welled up in her eyes. "I feel like such a fool, Fee."

Fiona shook her head and smiled. "Quinn, you're not a fool; you're just human. You just want to be loved, and there's nothing wrong with that. Unfortunately, you and I don't seem to be very good at choosing the right man for that."

Fiona tucked Quinn into bed that night, pulling the covers up snugly around her neck, the way she had so many times before, and Quinn had done the same for her. They would always mother each other in times like this. They always had.

Jack caught a cab back to the farm, where Fiona met him at the door with a hard look on her face, just daring him to say a word. She stood guard, her hands firmly planted on her hips while he hurriedly packed his bags and climbed back into the cab, which quickly sped out of the driveway.

Fiona watched the cab depart. Good riddance, she whispered, as she quietly closed the door.

CHAPTER 8

*Q*uinn felt she was making real progress with Megan Murphy. The young girl seemed to gain more self-confidence with every visit. She hadn't had a panic attack in over a month. Megan was intelligent and seemed to gain insight into her problems quickly. Her boyfriend, though, was still pressuring her to get married. Quinn was keen to know more about their relationship.

Megan described the start of their relationship as almost too romantic. They had met at a local pub after Thomas had moved to Ballyfrannen from Limerick City. That evening, as they sat in a corner booth, Thomas told her how beautiful she was and that he had never known anyone like her. From then on, he showered her with gifts and sent her flowers for every occasion, with loving messages attached. Nothing was too much or too good for his Megan, and he couldn't wait for them to be married.

Things had changed little by little in the months they had been dating. Thomas still professed to love her, but he became more controlling, always wanting to know where she was and who she was with when she wasn't with him and acting jealous if she spent time with friends. Still, she knew Thomas had a good heart. It was just that he loved her so much he couldn't bear to share her.

Quinn was more than a little concerned by Megan's description of her relationship with Thomas. She asked Megan if Thomas would accompany her on her next visit. Megan said she felt sure he wouldn't mind since he always asked her what they talked about and especially wanted to know if they talked about him.

Thomas arrived with Megan on her next visit and now sat nervously, jiggling his leg and biting his nails as he slumped in the chair. Quinn was not overly pleased with what she observed.

The boy reeked of stale cigarette smoke, and his unwashed hair was greasy, long, and unkempt. He appeared thin and unhealthy beneath his worn black leather jacket, tight jeans, and black t-shirt. His teeth were yellow and more than a little decayed.

Quinn had seen many young men like Thomas Lafferty, not just in Ireland but also in the States. She understood that life had dealt him one bad hand after another, and his history proved her right: drug-addicted, abusive father, neglectful mother, an older brother who was in prison for selling drugs.

Thomas had dropped out of school and left home at sixteen. He had lived on the streets for a few months before finally finding a low-paying job and moving into a tenement flat in one of the worst parts of Limerick City, which he shared with a couple of friends.

For the last few years, he had kicked around from one job to another. He was twenty-two and had recently moved from Limerick City to Ballyfrannen to seek employment. He had found a halfway decent job as a deliveryman for a brewery.

His real interest was computers, he said. There wasn't much he didn't know about them; according to him, only no tech company would give him a job because of his lack of education. Quinn couldn't help feeling sorry for him. How were people like Thomas ever supposed to climb out of the hole that family circumstances and life had left them in? Knowledge and insight were the only tools that could help this young man ever make any actual changes in his life. Quinn could give him those tools, but what he did with them would be up to him.

Thomas seemed cooperative as he answered Quinn's questions. He realized, he said, that he was a little too controlling with Megan, and he agreed to work on that. He made good eye contact when he spoke, and his answers were fairly articulate. Intelligence was a great thing when it came to changing your life. The more you understood your problems, the more you could change them.

Quinn was pleased with Megan and Thomas's session. As she sat making notes for their next visit, she couldn't help feeling more than a little hopeful that their outcome would be a good one.

Thomas Lafferty sat smoking a cigarette in his car, which was parked a few doors down from the Mental Health Clinic. He had dropped Megan off at work and then returned to spy on Megan's therapist. He could see her through the window that held those stupid potted plants. She sat at her desk with her back to the street. He chuckled to himself at how gullible the old cow had been. She had believed everything he'd said. He would happily sit in on Megan's visits and act as if he agreed with the old bag. She pretended to be so interested in helping Megan. What an act! She was just there to collect her pay cheque; that's all people like her cared about. He wasn't about to be fooled by the likes of her. But he would continue attending Megan's sessions; that way, he would know exactly what was going on.

It was lunchtime, and Quinn had eaten nothing all day.

She was famished and began thinking about what she would order as she stepped out of the clinic and headed towards Daily Kneads. Her mood was upbeat as she crossed the street and then ran straight into Colin Brodie. Quinn's brain turned to fudge. "Colin, oh, ah, I was just heading to Daily Kneads for a bite." Why had she said that?

"That's grand; I was just heading there myself. We can go together and share a table." Colin smiled down at her.

The day that had seemed so pleasant just a few moments ago now seemed destined to end in disaster. Quinn was sure she would make a complete fool of herself again in front of Colin. Already, having him so near was affecting her in every possible way.

"Shall we sit over here by the window, then?" Colin gestured towards what, until then, had been Quinn's favorite table in the little health food store.

"That's fine, Colin." Sure, why not? Quinn thought. I might as well sit where everyone can see me make a complete idiot of myself.

Quinn ordered soup, which seemed like the easiest and fastest choice. Her goal was to get out of there as quickly as possible.

Colin studied the plastic menu for what seemed an eternity before ordering a tuna sandwich.

Then, after smiling warmly at Quinn, he said, "I'm glad we ran into each other, Quinn. We didn't get a chance to get acquainted while I was working in your cottage. Maybe now we can get to know each other better?" His smile turned mischievous. "I would almost say you have been purposely avoiding me." Quinn opened her mouth to protest, but Colin continued in a more serious tone. "Quinn, have I offended you in some way? Because if I have…"

Quinn cut him off. "You have done nothing, Colin." Then

she paused, thinking carefully about what she would tell a patient to do in a similar circumstance.

Quinn glanced at Colin before continuing. "To be honest, I seem to turn into a tongue-tied schoolgirl whenever I'm around you, Colin Brodie."

There, she had said it. She could feel her face turning a bright crimson, and her heart felt like it would pound out of her chest. Now, he would see how pathetic she was. She would lose all credibility, but then, at least, he would leave her alone.

Colin sat for a long moment, looking at her with his head tilted slightly to the side, digesting this new information. Then he smiled, making Quinn go weak in the knees. Leaning towards her, he said, "That's the best news I've heard in a very long time." He sat back before adding, "Haven't you noticed I turn into a rather tongue-tied schoolboy myself whenever I'm around you, Quinn?"

With that, everything seemed to thaw between them. Finally, Quinn became comfortable in his presence, and they sat laughing and chatting throughout the rest of their lunch.

Quinn felt on top of the world as she parted with Colin and headed back toward the clinic. Just then, a car, which seemed to come out of nowhere, drove past Quinn at high speed, missing her by millimeters. By the time Quinn recovered herself, Colin was at her side.

"My God, Quinn, are you alright? I can't believe how close that car came to hitting you! Did you get the license plate number?"

"I'm fine, Colin. Really. I probably stepped out too soon. I still have trouble remembering to look right instead of left." Quinn could feel her heart pounding hard from the scare. "I think I'll just go back to the clinic and relax for a few minutes before my next patient arrives." Quinn's legs felt wobbly as she turned towards the clinic.

"Are you sure you don't want me to walk you over and sit with you for a while?"

The look of concern on Colin's face touched Quinn and also made her feel more relaxed. Feeling her old self again, she said more confidently, "I really am fine, Colin, but thanks for..." Quinn chuckled, "For everything, I guess." They both knew what she meant and when they parted this time, they were both smiling.

Quinn's next patient was Agnes Meek. It wasn't professional to have favorite clients, but all therapists did. They had least favorites, too, and Agnes fell into that category. Try as she might, Quinn could not seem to make any headway with Agnes. She began to wonder why Agnes bothered coming in at all. She didn't seem interested in making any genuine changes. Quinn knew her overeating would continue until she confronted her past.

Quinn adjusted her face into a pleasant and non-threatening expression as she saw Agnes heading down the hallway toward her office. She could hear the rustle of her clothes as her hips brushed against the walls on both sides of the narrow hallway. Her breathing came in quick puffs as she walked.

Agnes swooped into the office with a grand flourish, red-faced and slightly winded from the exertion. She sat across from Quinn and immediately began applying lip gloss to her brightly colored lips. Her hair looked freshly coiffed, and she smelled, again, of expensive perfume.

"Hello, Agnes, how was your week?" Quinn asked.

"My week was terrible. I've gained three more pounds! These sessions aren't helping one bit! I thought you were supposed to be good at your job?"

Quinn ignored the insults. "Agnes, I've told you that we have to examine your past if we want to find out why you overeat. Are you willing to start doing that today?"

"I don't know what you mean; my past is all we ever talk about. All you aim to do is ask me questions about my sister and how she died!" Agnes looked annoyed.

"Don't you think it's important we look at that and examine your relationship with your parents?" Quinn waited for Agnes to reply.

Agnes sat fuming for a few minutes. "Alright, let's do it your way. What do you want to know?" Agnes looked at Quinn in a guarded way.

"Why don't you tell me more about your family life? Maybe you could start by telling me about your mother. What was she like when you were little?" asked Quinn.

"My mother didn't feel good most of the time when I was young. She spent a lot of time lying on the sofa. My sister made her feel bad because she was so much trouble." Agnes spoke in a soft, almost childlike voice.

"Why was your sister so much trouble, do you think?" asked Quinn.

"Because she always wanted something. She wouldn't leave my mother alone. My mother needed her rest; she couldn't be chasing after a three-year-old all day long." Agnes widened her eyes and blinked rapidly as she spoke, as was her habit.

"But isn't it a mother's job to care for her children?" Quinn posed the question to Agnes.

"Children shouldn't be so much trouble. Emily was too much trouble. That's why my mother was always sad and in a bad mood." Agnes sighed and squirmed in her chair. Then she reached for her purse. "I don't like talking about my mother. Let's move on to something else." Agnes began rummaging through her expensive designer handbag, finally pulling out a compact and staring into its mirror as she began to methodically apply more blush to her already bright cheeks.

"We could talk about your father. What was he like when you were little, Agnes?"

Agnes brightened. "My Dad was funny. He made me laugh all the time. He would take me to the store and buy me ice cream. I would stand up next to him on the seat while he drove, and he would put his arm out when he slowed down so I wouldn't fall. I liked spending time with my father." Agnes paused momentarily and then added, "I miss him." She looked as though she were about to cry.

Quinn took the opening. "Couldn't you call your father and tell him you miss him?"

Agnes slammed the compact shut and turned on Quinn. "You don't know anything about anything, Little Miss Smarty Therapist!" With that, Agnes pulled herself up from the chair and stormed out of the room.

Well, that went well, thought Quinn, realizing she had the beginning of what would probably become a nasty headache. I might as well call it a day.

CHAPTER 9

Quinn's headache grew worse as she drove home, and by the time she arrived at the cottage, all she could think of was a cup of tea and a hot bath.

Fiona greeted her at the door, more excited than usual. "Quinn, have you been listening to the news? A psychologist was hacked to bits today in her office back in the States. A man just walked in with a cleaver and chopped her to death with it. Isn't that awful?"

Quinn knew Fiona was telling her this out of concern for her safety. For a second, Quinn thought back to the car that had almost run her down and then to the look in Agnes's eyes as she stormed out of the office. Now, her head was pounding. She needed to regroup and thought it was best to change the subject. "Fiona, you'll never guess who I had lunch with today!"

"Who?"

"Colin Brodie! And I think we're going to start seeing each other. What do you think about that?"

Fiona visibly brightened. "I think it's about bloody time; that's what I think!"

. . .

THE FOLLOWING DAY, Quinn was still feeling a bit off. The near miss with the car and then having Agnes Meek storm out of her office had upset her more than she realized. She smiled when she thought of Colin Brodie and their lunch yesterday. Could it be true that he might feel the same way about her as she did him?

Quinn began to prepare Maggie and Pike's breakfasts. Dry and canned dog food mixed for Maggie, and dry dog food with hard-boiled eggs, mashed and still in their shells, for Pike. She then sprinkled a few mealworms and sliced apples on top. He watched expectantly from his vantage point atop the refrigerator.

As Quinn sat one dish on the floor for Maggie and another on top of the refrigerator for Pike, someone knocked at the cottage's front door. Quinn peeked out a front window before going to the door. An attractive woman she didn't recognize was standing on the stoop. Quinn suddenly felt a little sheepish to still be in her nightclothes. A glance in the mirror that hung by the front door told Quinn her hair was sticking out in every possible direction. Great, just great, she thought. Quinn opened the door, feeling old and frumpy in her robe and slippers.

The woman appeared startled at Quinn's appearance and then regained her composure.

"Hello, my name is Madeleine Tricot. I am here to speak with the owner of this little farm. You are the owner, no?" She smiled expectantly at Quinn. "I was in town yesterday, and the girl who works at Daily Kneads, she point you out to me, and she say you were the woman who owns this cottage."

The woman was quite tall and spoke with a thick French accent. She looked to be about thirty-five or forty. Her shoulder-length hair was shiny, dark, and straight, and her makeup was expertly done. She had a good figure and, though dressed in a casual jumper and jeans, still looked sophisticated.

She continued speaking. "I am to be your new neighbor. My husband and I own the land next to yours. My husband, he is Bruno Tricot. You have heard of him, no? He is the famous French documentary filmmaker. He make the film, Blood in the Desert; you have heard of this film, no?"

Quinn opened her mouth to say something, but Madeleine continued speaking.

"Isn't it grand that we shall be neighbors! This is great news, no?" Madeleine smiled down at Quinn. Quinn cinched the belt of her robe a little tighter, not at all convinced that this was great news.

"I stopped by today to tell you we wish to purchase some of your land. It is the land to the west of your little cottage, the land with the old ruin. That parcel is about ten acres, no? My husband he is a great artist, and he needs his privacy. You understand this, no doubt? We will build a large stone fence right here," Madeleine Tricot motioned out the window towards a little tree about thirty feet from Quinn and Fiona's cottage, just on the other side of the stream. "That way, we shall both have the privacy, you see?" Madeleine Tricot smiled as though she thought Quinn would be delighted at the idea of a privacy fence that would cut her off from her beautiful little stream. "We will pay you twice what you paid for the land; this is very fair, no?"

Just as Quinn was about to speak, she saw Fiona standing in the sitting room doorway. Fiona was also in her robe and slippers, and her hair looked slightly worse than Quinn's.

We look like a matched set of furry, middle-aged book-ends, thought Quinn. She wondered how much of the conversation Fiona had heard, but she didn't have to wonder for long.

Fiona fairly exploded. "NO! We certainly will NOT be selling you any of our land! How dare you come into our home and demand such a thing? Who do you think you are, anyway?"

Madelein sighed, obviously annoyed. "I have told your friend who I am. I am Madeleine Tricot, and my husband is the famous film..."

"Oh, cut the crap about your husband being a famous filmmaker? I don't care if he's Louie the Fourteenth, you're not getting any of our land, and that's that." Fiona was as mad as Quinn had ever seen her.

Madeleine Tricot gasped with indignation. "Well, I should have known; you selfish Americans are all alike, always thinking of yourselves!"

Fiona's face had turned almost purple. She stepped closer to the woman. "Listen here, Frenchie, you get off our land right now, or I'll sic our raven on you."

Pike had flown in from the kitchen and was now perched on the coat rack near the front door. As though on cue, Pike lowered his head and gave a threatening caw in the direction of the French woman. Madeleine Tricot shrieked as she spotted the big bird and ran towards the front door. Fiona slammed the door after her and marched towards the kitchen.

"If that little Frenchie ever shows her face around here again, I'll snatch that dyed hair of hers right off her head!"

Quinn followed Fiona into the kitchen, where she had begun slamming cups and saucers onto the table, startling Maggie. She then slammed the teapot down on the stove for good measure.

"Can you believe the nerve of that woman, expecting us just to roll over and sell our land to her just because her husband happened to make some film or other? I'm surprised she didn't want us to vacate altogether. I hope we never have to see her again." Fiona stood with her hands on her hips.

"Well, if they really are going to build a house next to ours, we will most certainly see her again." Quinn found the thought genuinely depressing. Their cottage and little farm were such a refuge, and now to think that woman might be living next door. It wasn't pleasant to contemplate.

AFTER QUINN and Fiona had each completed their morning routine, they decided to drive into Ballyfrannen for lunch and shopping. It was Wednesday, the one day Quinn saw no patients at the clinic. They hoped the distraction would take their minds off the unpleasant experience of meeting the French woman.

"Look, Quinn, there's Colin's truck parked in front of the hardware store. Shall we stop in to say hi?"

Quinn thought that Fiona probably wanted to see Colin and her together so she could decide for herself how they were doing. However, she wasn't opposed to seeing Colin, so she agreed to stop at the hardware store.

As they entered the store, they saw Colin deep in conversation with a woman whose back was turned towards them.

Colin's face broke into a broad smile when he noticed Quinn and Fiona. "Quinn, how unexpectedly nice to see you. You too, Fiona."

Just then, the woman turned, and to their mutual horror, Quinn and Fiona found themselves facing the French woman they had chased from their door that morning.

Madeleine Tricot gasped as she realized who they were. "There they are! These are the two mad women I was telling you about, Colin. You will protect me from them, no?" She stepped closer to Colin and put her hand on his arm.

Colin looked down at the woman momentarily and then

began to laugh. "I guess I couldn't follow the conversation too closely because I didn't realize you were talking about Quinn and Fiona. You couldn't find two nicer people than these two women. Surely, there was some miscommunication because of the language barrier."

Looking at Fiona, Colin asked, "You didn't really throw this woman out of your house, did you, Fiona?"

"Yes, I did, and I'll do it again if she ever steps foot on my property!" Fiona glared menacingly at the French woman, who now stood even closer to Colin and still clutched his arm.

"What could she have done to make you so angry?" asked Colin, looking genuinely bewildered.

"Well, for starters, she wants to buy a large piece of our land and put a stone wall around it. It seems her husband needs his privacy because he is a great artist or something," said Fiona mockingly.

Colin asked Madeleine if she would excuse him for a moment, and taking Quinn and Fiona each by the arm, he walked with them to the front of the store. "I'm surprised at you two." Colin was smiling, but his face looked perplexed.

"Madeleine and her husband will build a lovely, large house on the land adjoining yours, and I'm sure you will enjoy having them as neighbors. They are two of the most interesting people you could ever meet. Bruno is a famous documentary filmmaker in France and has even won awards in the States for his work. Madeleine used to be a model and was on the cover of some very famous magazines before she retired to marry Bruno. It will be a real feather in our cap to have them here in Ballyfrannen. I feel honored to be building them a house."

"So, Colin, you think we should just sell them part of our farm out of gratitude for having them as neighbors?" Quinn thought maybe she didn't really know Colin Brodie at all.

"Of course not, Quinn, I didn't mean that. I just thought you and Fiona would be happy to have such a famous and well-respected couple as your neighbors. I knew nothing about them wanting to buy your land until now."

Quinn didn't know whether she believed Colin, but she knew she'd rather avoid standing in the middle of the hardware store talking about it with that dreadful woman looking on.

Fiona had clammed up completely, the way she always did when she felt hurt or misunderstood. She stood off a little to one side, ignoring everyone. Seeing this, Quinn felt even angrier with Colin. "Come on, Fiona, we're getting out of here."

Well, so much for a romance with Colin Brodie, thought Quinn as she and Fiona drove out of town, neither feeling like having lunch nor shopping anymore.

Colin phoned several times over the following days and left messages, but Quinn didn't return any of his calls. Maybe she just didn't trust men anymore, she thought. Certainly, her experiences with Jack Wyatt hadn't helped any in that department.

CHAPTER 10

Q uinn sat in her pleasant office at the clinic, waiting
for her next patient. She was finding her small
practice in Ballyfrannen to be very fulfilling. Cathal
had become a good friend, and Quinn had found him
competent and caring as director of the little clinic. She had
also made friends with the two other therapists who worked
there. All in all, it was a very satisfactory arrangement. She
could keep her own schedule and see only as many patients
as she chose, which left her with lots of time to spend at the
farm on various enterprises.

After years of neglect, Quinn, and Fiona enjoyed bringing
the farm back to life. They had finished restoring most of the
outbuildings. After that, they invested in a small tractor and
cleared out a good amount of undergrowth and debris built
up through the years.

Now, they felt they were ready to add some farm animals
and hoped to purchase a couple of pigs. They certainly had
room for them, and it seemed a shame to have all those
well-restored outbuildings on their property and not use
them. They had researched the different breeds of pigs and

finally settled on the ancient Oxford Sandy and Blacks, sometimes called the "Plum Pudding" or "Oxford Forest Pig." That breed of pig had existed in Britain for two or three hundred years, and they were the traditional pigs of farmers and cottagers. People said they possessed excellent temperaments and were wonderful mothers. They were also prolific and hardy, and since they were colored pigs with good coats, they were far less prone to sunburn. The breeder who raised them said that those were excellent pig qualities. They were the perfect choice for a first-time smallholder, he said.

His farm was in Oxfordshire, Britain, so the pigs would have to be shipped to Ireland. He had a litter of twelve piglets that were five months old and ready to be separated from their mother. The breeder suggested they take at least two piglets, as pigs were prone to melancholy and might die from loneliness without another pig around. Pigs were most bonded to their littermates, so choosing two from the same litter would be ideal. Quinn and Fiona hoped they were ready for such an endeavor. They would discuss it again tonight and decide before all the little piglets were spoken for.

Turning her mind back to her patients, Quinn got up from her desk and began watering the geraniums on the windowsill. She also replaced the empty box of tissues that sat on the small table next to the patient's chair. Today, she would see Megan Murphy and then Jozef Abram.

Megan came in alone, looking disheveled and upset. Quinn could tell she had been crying. She handed her a tissue and asked, "What's happened, Megan?"

"I've fought with my mum, is all, Dr. Langston. I want to move out of the house and find a flat with Thomas. Not get married yet; live with him for a bit first, but my mother is having none of it. She thinks I'm too young, and that Thomas is a loser, and that I'll be making the same mistakes she made at my age."

Quinn agreed with Megan's mother but knew better than to say so. "What do you think, Megan?"

"I think she should stay out of my business; that's what I think! She wasn't around when I was growing up, so why start being a parent now?"

Quinn felt this was a little harsh, given her mother's circumstances, but, again, she felt it best not to say so, saying instead, "I think it's hard for parents to let go of their children sometimes, especially if they have made bad choices themselves. Do you think it could be that your mother is just afraid for you right now?"

"Oh, I suppose so, but I'm still going to move in with Thomas, and that's that."

Megan had a look in her eye that told Quinn there was no use arguing.

The rest of the session passed with Quinn, giving Megan more tools to help with her anxiety. She taught her about deep breathing and mental imaging. These techniques helped relax the body. Quinn hoped that this new stress wouldn't cause Megan to resume having panic attacks.

Megan got up to leave. As she walked past Quinn's chair, she bent down and gave Quinn a hard little hug. "I wish my mum was more like you, Dr. Langston. If you have kids, they sure are lucky to have you as their mum. Do you have kids, Dr. Langston?"

Quinn rarely discussed her personal life with her patients, but Megan's comments touched her. "No, I don't have any children, Megan, just a growing assortment of animals."

Megan smiled and walked out of the office.

. . .

JOZEF ABRAM ARRIVED for his appointment ten minutes late and in a dark mood. Quinn was having a hard time getting him to talk at all. He sat in the chair, slumped over, with his head in his hands, mumbling what sounded like Polish swear words under his breath.

Quinn sighed, wondering why more patients couldn't be like Megan. That was silly, of course. She was there to help anyone who needed it. She decided to take a different approach with Jozef.

"Jozef, have you ever heard of inner child work?" It was an old therapy but an effective one for some patients.

"I have no idea what you are talking about." Jozef didn't bother to raise his head from his hands.

"Jozef, look at me for a moment and imagine that the little boy you once were is still inside you. Can you do that?"

Jozef finally looked up, "I can do that, I guess."

"Now, tell me what that little boy is doing right this minute."

"What do you mean, what he is doing? There is no little boy."

"But if there were a little boy, little Jozef, what would he be doing right now?"

Jozef considered for a long moment. "That boy, he would be getting a belt across his back; his mother, she would be hitting him. He would be scared because he would never know why she would hit him, why she was so mad all the time, and he would be crying. Then, his mother would tell him to go sit on the chair. Her eyes would have the hard look in them, like she cared nothing for him. Like she enjoyed what she was doing. He would never dare to disobey. He would sit on the wooden kitchen chair she kept against the wall in the far corner of the room, and he would still be crying and wondering what he did wrong. It was always the same every day; that was that little boy's life." Jozef again put his head in his hands.

Quinn wasn't surprised by Jozef's story. She understood Jozef's anger towards women well. Why wouldn't he be angry after being treated that way by the one woman who was supposed to protect and love him? Now, it was left to the other women in Jozef's life to endure the consequences of that woman's actions. The people who paid for the damage inflicted in childhood were usually not the guilty parties.

Quinn worked with Jozef for the rest of the hour, teaching him how to comfort his inner child. At first, Jozef found the whole concept ridiculous, but by the end of the session, he seemed to master the idea pretty well.

Quinn drove home with a heavy heart. Why didn't schools teach good parenting right alongside everything else? What could be more important than learning, at a young age, how to treat others with empathy? How many problems in this world could be solved if that ever happened?

LATER THAT NIGHT, after more discussion, Quinn and Fiona called the breeder to proceed with the purchase of the Oxford Sandy and Black piglets. The breeder in Oxfordshire said he would ship them within the week.

Margaret stopped by the following day after finishing her breakfast chores at the B&B. Her cheeks were flushed, as usual, and her short, wiry, red hair seemed to hover a little above her head, having a mind of its own, no matter how many times she patted it down. The three sat companionably around the large kitchen table, drinking tea and enjoying the homemade sweet rolls Margaret's mother had baked earlier that morning. Not surprisingly, Margaret had become one of their dearest friends and the person they always turned to for advice. Quinn and Fiona were eager to discuss their decision to buy the piglets with her.

Margaret took a sip of tea and then sat her cup down with a bit of a flourish, then she looked at the women. "Now, just so I have it, you're spending a small fortune on some fancy piglets that have to be shipped all the way from England just to keep as pets, is that it?" Margaret looked doubtful.

Quinn recited again from the literature the breeder had sent. "Margaret, they're one of the rarest and oldest English breeds. They probably date back to the seventeenth century. They're good foragers, too. Oh, and they don't easily sunburn because of their thick coats."

Margaret got that look on her face that was unique to the Irish. A cross between being both somber and amused at the same time. She patted her hair and took another long, deliberate sip of tea before speaking.

"Well, so ... I can't say sunburned pigs has ever been to great problem here in Ireland." Margaret sat back in her chair and tucked her chin as though she had imparted a sizeable amount of wisdom.

Fiona wasn't the least bit put off. "They're said to be excellent mothers. That's a good thing, isn't it?"

"You intend to breed them, then?"

"No, we're buying two females from the same litter," responded Quinn, who was beginning to feel a little foolish.

"Sows," corrected Margaret, and then, after a pause, "Well, then." Margaret squinted her eyes and looked up at the ceiling, the way she always did when she thought they were daft but was too polite to say so. Like most real farmers, Margaret was unsentimental when it came to animals. She couldn't wrap her mind around anyone wanting pigs as pets, especially expensive pigs that had to be shipped all the way from England. In Margaret's mind, pigs were only good for pork roasts or rashers. Anything else was just nonsense.

"Margaret, did you know you can housebreak a pig?" Fiona sipped her tea and waited for a reaction.

"Ah, go on with ye! You'll never be keepin' them in the house!" Margaret looked truly dismayed

Quinn and Fiona both laughed. "Actually, we were hoping Daniel would help us set up one of the outbuildings for them," said Quinn.

"He would, a' course," said Margaret, relaxing a little. "Now, tell me about this French lady that ye and our man Pike here ran off the property."

Fiona launched into the whole sordid encounter with Madeleine Tricot. Margaret sat sipping her tea, round-eyed with expectation, and occasionally exclaiming, "She never did!" to some of the more outrageous proposals of the now disdained Madeleine Tricot.

When Fiona finished, Margaret slammed her hand down forcefully on the kitchen table, which startled Maggie and caused Pike to vacate his perch atop the refrigerator. "I've never heard such cheek. I'll not be any friend to that woman, that's for sure!" Margaret sniffed indignantly and patted her hair. With that, they moved on to more pleasant subjects.

Daniel came the next day to help Fiona prepare one of the outbuildings for the new piglets. He explained that the large, low shed that stood the furthest from the cottage had been a piggery, as they were called in Ireland. Of course, they would need a fenced space outside the shed, so together, they made a large enclosure at the front of the piggery. They made sure the piglets would have plenty of room to roam.

Daniel shared all his knowledge regarding pigs, which was considerable. Fiona took notes, and when he mentioned being glad they were getting two, as one pig alone could become so depressed as to be prone to suicide, Fiona remembered what the breeder had said about the loneliness of one pig, and even though he hadn't called a pig dying of loneliness suicide, what else was it? One of the things Fiona loved about the Irish was the way they called a thing what it was and didn't sugarcoat it. Being that way herself, Fiona found it to be an admirable quality.

Fiona stood observing Daniel as he worked on a section of the enclosure. He had the body of a man used to hard work but was now beginning to settle into middle age, with just a hint of softness around the middle. His face was attractive in that its countenance was that of a man who bore no living creature any malice. He had reddish hair like his sister, but his was thick and curly. Fiona had to admit there was a certain grace about Daniel that she found very appealing.

During one of their morning chats around the kitchen table, Margaret told Fiona and Quinn about the only time Daniel had ever been in love and why, she supposed, he had never married.

She said that when Daniel was twenty; he had taken some agricultural courses at the university in Cork City. There he'd met a young woman. Margaret said Daniel was immediately smitten, and the young woman seemed to feel the same way about him. They dated for several months, and then, just as Daniel was thinking about marriage, he saw her leaving her dorm, hand in hand, with another man. Heartbroken, Daniel asked her for an explanation, and she'd told him that, although she cared for him, she could never marry someone who intended to spend his life in the country. She had bigger plans for her life; she said. Soon after, she married an American and moved to New York City. Margaret thought Daniel feared that no woman would be content with his simple farm life, so he abandoned the idea of marriage.

Fiona thought back to her marriage. She had met Nick Rossi on her twenty-first birthday when Quinn and a group of friends had taken her to a local hangout to celebrate. Seeing the balloons and gifts, Nick walked past their table and stopped to wish Fiona happy birthday. Fiona and Nick hit it off immediately. They spent the rest of the evening together, and by the time Fiona allowed him to take her home, she was sure she was in love.

At Nick's suggestion, she dropped out of college and took a position as an office assistant in an insurance office, a job she hated. Quinn had begged her not to marry Nick, but, of course, she hadn't listened. Nick turned out to be a smooth-talking ladies' man with a double standard regarding marriage. He could do whatever he pleased, but he expected Fiona to be the traditional, long-suffering wife who tended to his every need. What made it even worse was that no matter how much Fiona tried to please him, he always found something to criticize. Her hair was too short, the house wasn't clean enough, or she wasn't a good enough cook. And he hated plants, the one thing in life that gave her the most joy. He wouldn't allow her to have a single one in the house; he was allergic to anything green, he said.

Finally, after one too many nights of coming home late with lipstick on his shirt, Fiona kicked him out. Soon after, with a small loan from the bank, she started Bloomers, which became a massive success thanks to her love of anything that grew in the ground. Fiona, like Quinn, had never remarried, having instead a series of fairly disastrous love affairs in the ensuing years. She had never regained her self-esteem where men were concerned, and Quinn usually disapproved of her choices. Quinn felt she continued to pick men who would mistreat her in one way or another. Fiona had to admit that she was right.

Fiona was enjoying Daniel's company more and more. They seemed to value each other in a way that was new to Fiona when it came to men. Theirs was turning into a deep friendship, but she was hesitant to call it more, as Daniel had none of the qualities she usually looked for in the opposite sex. Fiona listed these qualities: outgoing (Daniel certainly was not), the life of the party (Daniel at a party seemed absurd), charming (Daniel had a quiet kind of charm). He was funny, too, in his way. His humor was low-key, but he could make her laugh harder than anyone she had ever met. Fiona wasn't given to over-analyzing, though, so she was satisfied to accept things as they were.

Another time when Fiona and Daniel were outback, Daniel walked into the smallest of the farm's sheds. "Fiona, you've got to see this! I've just found a trove of old tools — they must be over a hundred years old!"

Fiona froze. Fear of a particular kind gripped her, and she began to back up. Daniel poked his head out, and seeing her distress, rushed to her side.

"What is it, Fiona? What has happened?" Daniel had a look of genuine concern on his face. Fiona looked up into his kind eyes and then told him something that she rarely spoke about with anyone.

When Fiona was four years old, some older boys in her neighborhood had, as a joke, locked her in an old refrigerator that was in her neighbor's basement. The boys were young, only seven or eight, and hadn't understood the danger they were putting Fiona in. They had gone out to play, leaving her alone in the locked refrigerator. Terrified, Fiona screamed to be let out, but no one had heard. Finally, the boys began to feel guilty and came back to tell Fiona they were sorry, but when they opened the refrigerator, they found her curled up in a ball, unconscious from lack of oxygen. One of the boy's parents called an ambulance, and they rushed Fiona to the hospital.

There had been no lasting harm done, as the boys had, luckily, gone back just in time, but psychologically, the experience had left Fiona unable to deal with small spaces. She was so claustrophobic that the thought of being in even a small shed was enough to make her almost dizzy with fear.

While Fiona was explaining all this to Daniel, he stood looking at her intently. When she had finished, he reached down and gently touched her chin, cupping it with the palm of his hand. "Poor lass," he said. "I wish I had been there to save you from such a memory."

Fiona felt a strange sensation. She realized that never in her life had a man been this kind to her. She smiled at the thought that she might be falling in love with Daniel.

THE FOLLOWING WEEK, Quinn and Fiona drove to Cork City Airport to pick up their piglets. They discussed names as they drove home with the two little creatures tucked safely in the back seat, with the seat belt stretched across their traveling crate. They finally decided on Hilda for the larger one and Tam for the smaller one, who was also the more spotted of the two.

Quinn and Fiona stood watching the little piglets as they explored their new home. Daniel had done an excellent job with the large enclosure, and the piglets seemed delighted to be in this new environment. They ran through the grass, snorting and grunting as they sniffed at the ground. They surprised Quinn and Fiona with their agility and speed. Who knew pigs were athletic?

Maggie ran around the perimeter of the enclosure, barking excitedly, and stooping down with her backside in the air, hoping to entice the piglets into a game of chase. Pike sat regally on a post, casting a disdainful eye toward the new creatures. Finally, jealous of all the attention, he swooped in and gave the smallest one, Tam, a peck with his beak. This sent both piglets running into the piggery amidst a frenzy of squeals. Quinn gave Pike a look that said, never do that again, and Pike, indignant at the reprimand, flew into a nearby tree, where he sat perched on a high branch, pretending to ignore everyone.

After a few days, Pike made friends with the newcomers, finally realizing that their mealtime meant new titbits for him. He would fly into their enclosure and perch on the edge of their large bowl while they, grateful to have made peace with this powerful creature, shared their meal with him. Soon, Pike considered them a part of his flock and, as such, his responsibility, so he flew over their enclosure on his daily patrols.

CHAPTER 11

*Q*uinn drove down the narrow country road that led to Ballyfrannen, deep in thought, thinking about her patients. Suddenly, she was startled out of her reverie by a car approaching fast behind her. Quinn, not being a fast driver herself, moved her car further toward the left to let them pass. As a silver car pulled alongside, Quinn saw the driver was wearing a hat pulled down low over their face; she couldn't tell whether it was a man or a woman.

Just as she registered how odd that was, the car suddenly swerved hard, almost bumping the back passenger door. Quinn gasped in surprise and stepped on the brakes. The other car slowed with her, though, and swerved into her side again. Quinn turned the wheel as hard as she could, narrowly escaping being hit. She was in a panic to get away from the other car, but how? To her left lay a rocky slope leading down to the bay. The other car's driver kept edging her over, little by little until she was in danger of pitching down the side of the steep decline. Finally, in desperation, Quinn pushed the accelerator to the floor and managed to get in front of the other vehicle. Quinn's Volvo handled the narrow, curving roads well, and she now realized she could outmaneuver the other car.

She drove as fast as she dared, keeping watch in her rearview mirror until realizing they had finally given up and turned onto another road.

Once in town, Quinn pulled her car to the side of the road. She was still breathing hard, and her heart was banging in her chest. She took some deep breaths as the realization set in that someone had just tried to kill her. Why? And more importantly, who? Quinn remembered the incident in town when someone had almost run her down. Hadn't that been a silver car, too? Quinn was almost sure it had. Should she go to the Garda and tell them what had just happened? What could she tell them, though? She hadn't seen the driver and couldn't even say whether it was a man or a woman. Quinn had never been good at makes and models of cars, either, and she wasn't at all sure she could identify the car again if she saw it. It had all happened so fast, and it had taken so much concentration just to stay on the road.

Quinn decided that the best course of action was to do some investigating on her own. She needed to figure out who might want to do her harm and who among the people she came in contact with owned a silver car.

QUINN FELT CALMER as she sat in her office waiting for Agnes Meek. Her appointment was at ten o'clock. Agnes arrived on time, as polished and coiffed as ever but a bit more subdued than usual. Quinn took a few more deep breaths before beginning.

"Hello Agnes, it's good to see you."

"It's good to see you too, Dr. Langston." Agnes had a

sincere look on her face. "I want to apologize for the way I ran out of here last time. Talking about my family must make me nervous, but I can't think why that would be. Anyway, I apologize for the way I acted. I'll talk about whatever you want today. By the way, I've lost five pounds; isn't that wonderful? This week, I just wasn't in the mood to eat for some reason."

"That is incredible news, Agnes! Maybe talking about your family helped you a bit? By that, I mean reducing your need to overeat. Agnes, some people use food to repress their emotions in the same way that other people use alcohol or drugs. Do you think you overeat to keep from feeling unpleasant feelings?"

Quinn tried to keep her voice as soothing as possible, hoping that this idea wouldn't have the effect of setting Agnes off again.

Agnes sat for a moment as though considering Quinn's words.

"You know, you may have a point. Dr. Langston, maybe my childhood wasn't as great as I make it out to be."

It was always such a remarkable feeling for a therapist when a patient experienced some insight into their problems. Quinn and Agnes spent the rest of the hour gently probing the edges of Agnes' true feelings regarding her childhood.

Quinn sat back in her chair after the session, feeling exhilarated. Agnes was finally making some progress. She admitted it wasn't normal for a mother to resent the care of her children, and she hadn't rejected the idea that her mother might have been suffering from a deep depression for most of her life.

Still feeling optimistic about her session with Agnes, Quinn rose and walked to the window to see if the geraniums needed watering. She gently felt the soil in the pot with her fingers as she idly looked out the window; just then, Agnes Meek climbed into a silver Mercedes parked across the street from the clinic, and with a big smile on her face, quickly drove away.

Quinn gasped and sank back down into her chair. Had Agnes been the one trying to kill her this morning?

CHAPTER 12

*M*egan came in for her eleven o'clock appointment looking much happier than she had the week before. Quinn, though, couldn't concentrate on anything Megan said.

Finally, having noticed Quinn's preoccupation, Megan asked, "Dr. Langston, are you alright? You look quite pale. You aren't coming down with something, are you?"

Quinn appreciated the girl's concern, "I'm fine, Megan, really. I just had a scare earlier in my car, that's all."

"The roads around this part of Cork can be dangerous, that's for sure," responded Megan. "You should be real careful, Dr. Langston; I wouldn't want anything to happen to my favorite therapist."

They both laughed, and Quinn tried to be more attentive throughout the rest of the session.

On the drive home, Quinn felt herself constantly looking into the rearview mirror as though expecting the silver car to appear behind her again at any moment. She had decided not to tell anyone about her experience that morning. She knew she would only worry Fiona by telling her, and anyway, what good would it do? This was something Quinn planned to deal with herself. Tomorrow was her day off, and she would investigate who might own a silver car beside Agnes Meek. She also wanted to find out all she could about Agnes' personal life and that of Jozef Abram. Jozef could quite possibly be transferring his angry feelings onto Quinn as his therapist, being unable, as yet, to feel them towards his mother. She wasn't ruling out Thomas Lafferty as a possibility, either. He seemed cooperative, but she couldn't be sure whether he was sincere, and he came from a violent background. He was so possessive of Megan. Likewise, he might see Quinn's relationship with her as a threat. She also was keen to know more about her new neighbor, Madeleine Tricot. She seemed like someone who would do almost anything to get what she wanted. Maybe she was trying to scare Quinn into selling the farm to her and her famous husband. Quinn's fear hardened into anger. Whoever it was had a surprise coming if they thought they could intimidate her. Quinn remembered again just how much she hated bullies.

The next morning, Quinn sat in Cathel Fagin's office with her hands wrapped around a cup of hot tea. She was finding it hard to stay warm after yesterday's experience with the silver car.

Cathel sat at his desk wearing the calm expression of a well-trained psychologist. The fingers of one hand silently drummed his desk as he waited to see why Quinn had sought him out. He was a slightly built man, very non-threatening and studious-looking. Quinn guessed him to be about thirty-five. He wore small wire-rimmed glasses. His sandy-colored hair was thinning a bit at the temples. He radiated kindness and understanding and was, therefore, just the person Quinn felt like being with just now.

Cathel would also be just the person to ask about Agnes

Meek. He had lived his whole life in Ballyfrannen. He should know a lot about the people there.

After some chit-chat, Quinn asked Cathel what he knew about her patient. Cathel sat back in his chair and slipped off his glasses, rubbing his fingers on either side of his nose before responding.

"I think the Meeks left Ballyfrannen about twenty years ago. I was a teenager then, but I remember them a little, and I remember my parents talking about them. They were always a bit odd. The family kept to themselves. When Agnes was young, the Meeks lost another daughter in an accident. I think she drowned or something. Anyway, they treated Agnes like shite after that." Cathel looked up to see if he had offended Quinn with his language. She smiled in response.

"I guess they blamed Agnes for her sister's death, which was ridiculous since she was just a small child herself at the time. She was a bit of a lost soul from then on, and even more so after her parents left town, leaving her behind. She was older than me, but I remember seeing her around. The girl was as thin as a rail back then, with loads of freckles and long, stringy, almost orange-colored hair. She had that vacant look in her eyes, too, like she had forgotten something and was trying to recall what it was. After she left school, she worked at one of the pubs waiting tables. Then she won the lottery a few years back, and of course that changed everything."

"She did a real makeover on herself and bought a big house and a fancy car. She also began turning her nose up at everyone in Ballyfrannen. That lost her what few friends she had. Soon, she started putting on weight and—well, you see what's happened to her, I guess."

Quinn thanked Cathel for the information and then headed across the street to Daily Kneads. She had invited Colin Brodie to lunch to see if she could garner more information regarding the Tricots. As awkward as she felt having to see Colin again, she was sure he would know the most about the French couple, as he'd been spending so much time with Madeleine designing their house.

Colin sat waiting for Quinn at the front table by the window in Daily Kneads. She could see him through the glass as she approached. He was wearing a khaki-colored shirt and a wool jacket of the same color. Quinn noticed that the color suited him very well. She was embarrassed to realize how hard her heart was pounding as she entered the little health food store.

Colin felt nervous as he watched Quinn walk across the street toward the cafe. He was grateful, though, that at least she was no longer angry with him. He couldn't help noticing how her fitted black jumper and well-cut jeans flattered her figure.

'Careful, man,' he told himself. 'Don't chase her off again by saying anything stupid, like how beautiful she looks or how much you've missed her. Let her do the talking and see which way the wind is blowing. That way, you'll be less likely to put a foot wrong.' Colin sat up a little straighter and cleared his throat in preparation.

Quinn sat down, feeling a little breathless. She smiled at Colin and breathed deeply, collecting her thoughts before speaking. Then, she noticed Colin's hands on the table. Such nice hands. Her eyes wandered up his muscular arms and onto his face. Such an extraordinary face. And... 'Quinn, get a grip on yourself for heaven's sake,' she told herself, and then, out loud, she said, "Thank you again, Colin, for meeting me on such short notice."

"I can't think of anyone I'd rather be having lunch with, Quinn."

Colin cursed himself mentally, as he was sure that was the wrong thing to say. Why couldn't he manage his words better?

Quinn relaxed a little and gave Colin a very flirtatious smile. "I can't think of anyone I would rather be having lunch with, either." Quinn then hesitantly approached the subject of the Tricots.

"Colin, how well do you know the French couple?"

The question made Colin nervous. Things were going so well. He wanted to avoid saying anything that would make Quinn angry with him again. He still wasn't sure exactly what had happened in the hardware store to upset Quinn, but he didn't want a repeat performance, so he chose his words carefully.

"I met Bruno and Madeleine about three weeks ago when they scheduled an appointment to see me at my office. They said they had purchased the land next to your farm and wanted to start planning a house there and begin building as soon as possible. Madeleine said it would be a retreat for Bruno since he usually lived such a fast-paced life, traveling to different parts of the world and making movies.

To tell you the truth, they both spoke with such thick accents that it was all I could do to understand them. Bruno has returned to France for a few weeks, but I still have a great deal of trouble understanding Madeleine. I didn't get the whole story about how she had stopped at your farm that morning and, more or less, demanded you and Fiona sell her part of your land."

"When you didn't return my calls, I called Fiona, and she filled me in on all the details of Madeleine's visit. I'm deeply sorry if I seemed less than sympathetic at the hardware store that day, Quinn. For the record, I think Madeleine's behavior was outrageous. I would never condone behavior like that, especially towards you and Fiona."

Quinn appreciated Colin's apology. She was beginning to feel like she had overreacted a little that day. Seeing Madeleine Tricot's hand on Colin's arm hadn't helped the situation, she was sure. Maybe they could start over with their relationship, but right now, she needed to ask him a few more questions about the French couple.

"Colin, do you remember when exactly Madeleine's husband left town, and—I know this sounds silly, but do you know what color car Madeleine drives?"

Colin began to feel concerned. Why was Quinn asking such odd questions about the Tricots?

"Quinn, is there more to this than you're telling me? Have the Tricots threatened you in any way?"

Quinn decided to tell Colin about the incident with the silver car. When she had finished, Colin sat back in his chair and exclaimed,

"My God, Quinn, why didn't you tell me about this sooner? When you put that together with the fact that someone tried to run you down, you can only conclude that someone means you real harm. I can't think the Tricots want your land badly enough to murder you for it, but then, I don't know either of them that well. Is there anyone else you can think of who might want to harm you? What about your patients—are any of them capable of something like this, do you think?"

"Oh, and to answer your question, Bruno left right after our first meeting. He said he would leave the details to Madeleine. He's a lot older than she is, by the way, about twenty years or so, I would guess from the look of him. And as for their car, it's a light grey Audi. I suppose a grey car could look silver in the sunshine. Yesterday was a sunny day. Quinn, have you spoken to the Garda about this?"

Colin took hold of Quinn's hand. His face had such a tender look of concern. Quinn felt tears well up and begin to slide down her cheeks. She had been holding in a lot of emotion since yesterday morning, she realized, and now, with Colin holding on tightly to her hand, it was finally coming out.

Quinn reached into her bag for a tissue and began dabbing at her eyes just as the waitress approached to take their order. She was the same young girl who had been there the first day Quinn and Fiona sat at this table watching the old men carry Orla Coughlin's coffin to the church.

Bridget Madden was the niece of the owner of Daily Kneads and the daughter of Liam Madden, the very same who had sold her and Fiona their farm. Quinn knew Bridget well now. She knew she was working to help pay her way through university and that she was studying to be an estate agent, like her father.

Seeing Quinn's distress, Bridget placed her hand solicitously on Quinn's shoulder and scowled at Colin. "Colin Brodie, have you nothing better to do with your time than to make a good woman cry?"

This simple act of kindness caused Quinn to cry even harder as she remembered why she had settled in this wonderful little town. She was determined that no one would drive her out of her hard-won life here in Ballyfrannen.

Quinn tried to compose herself as she reached to pat Bridget's hand. She assured the girl that Colin had not been the reason for her tears. Bridget seemed less than convinced as she took their order and, with one last stern glance at Colin, headed back behind the counter.

Quinn answered Colin's question regarding the Garda. "I didn't think I had enough information to take to the police yet, Colin. What could I tell them? They might think I was just an American overreacting to driving on the left side of the road or looking in the wrong direction when crossing the street. I don't even know whether it was a man or a woman driving or the make or model of the car either, for that matter."

"You can't just sit back and wait for something else to happen, Quinn; you have to do something." Colin could not hide his feelings as he looked across the table at Quinn.

"You're right, of course, but I am doing something. I'm trying to find out all I can about anyone who might have a grudge against me for any reason. I'm sure you know, Colin, that as a therapist, I can't discuss my patients with you, but I am looking into the backgrounds of several of them to see if I can discover more about who they are."

"People only tell you what they want you to know, even in psychotherapy, and it is possible to miss the mark knowing what kind of person you're dealing with. A sociopath, for example, may seem kind and empathetic and excel at convincing even a trained therapist that's truly who they are. Sociopaths even use therapy to learn how to be more convincing at mimicking empathetic behavior. They want you to see a kind and caring human being when, of course, that's not at all who they are. The very definition of a sociopath is someone incapable of having those feelings. Sociopaths are people who literally have no conscience."

Colin looked truly frightened now, which Quinn found touching, but she wanted to avoid discussing the situation further. She chose to lighten the mood. She spent the rest of their lunch entertaining Colin with stories of Hilda and Tam and how Pike and Maggie got on with the pair. Before they parted outside the health food store, Colin took her arm and softly kissed her cheek.

Quinn walked away with a little smile on her face as she thought about the kiss. Her thoughts soon turned back to the situation she was in, though. Quinn wondered again about Jozef Abram and Thomas Lafferty. She needed to find out more without making either of them suspicious, but not today, she decided. She had done enough investigating for one day. All she wanted to do now was go home to her little cottage and be with Fiona and her animals. She tried not to look in the rearview mirror constantly, but she was finding it impossible not to do so. This was no way to live, she thought, and the sooner she sorted this out, the better.

CHAPTER 13

*T*he next morning, Quinn drove to the clinic, with a knot in her stomach. She still felt nervous and was relieved to find a parking spot at the back of the small building. Today's work would be light. Only Megan Murphy was on the schedule. Quinn wondered if Thomas would be with Megan this time. The thought made her uncomfortable, but she knew she needed to hide her feelings and continue as though nothing was bothering her.

Quinn stuck her head into the waiting room a few minutes before nine. Megan sat on one of the hard plastic chairs, chewing her fingernails. Thomas sat next to her, quietly reading a magazine. Quinn quickly slapped a smile on her face and greeted them as they headed toward her office.

Megan seemed in an especially good mood, and even Thomas seemed a little happier and more relaxed than usual. They wasted no time in telling Quinn that they had moved in together. They had rented a little flat above a pub in town called Timothy McCoog's. It catered to the younger crowd, so there would be loud music until the wee hours, but being young themselves, that didn't bother them at all. It was only a bedsit, which meant one room with a pull-down bed, but the rent was cheap, and Megan was finally out of the house. They were together, and that was all that mattered, they said.

The session passed uneventfully. Megan said the panic attacks were no longer a problem, and in fact, she was happier than she had ever been.

Thomas, who had seemed interested in understanding some of his control issues a few sessions back, now allowed Quinn to explore those issues more fully.

Quinn explained how low self-esteem and feelings of not having control of your life could lead to wanting to control others. Thomas seemed to grasp the concepts very well, and Quinn was again impressed with Thomas's intelligence. Intelligence could be used for good or evil, though. Many murderers were highly intelligent individuals.

Quinn brought her mind back around to what Thomas was saying. He was asking her about a book she had mentioned a few sessions back that might be of interest to him. Quinn rose to pull the book from the little bookshelf she had brought from home to house some of the books she liked to share with her patients. It was "The Power of Positive Thinking" by Norman Vincent Peale. Quinn had read it herself when she was young, and it had changed her life. She truly hoped it would be of value to Thomas.

Quinn's next patient was a middle-aged British woman named Sylvia Watson. This was her first visit. Quinn was glad for the distraction of a new patient. She made mental notes as the woman walked into her office and took a seat.

Sylvia Watson seemed nervous as she cast her eyes about the small room, and there was just a hint of arrogance in the way she adjusted herself in the chair. Her eyes were dark and small, almost fox-like, and her face was narrow and pinched and wore a slight sneer. Sylvia gave a false little laugh before saying, "Good gracious, this is a small room, isn't it?"

"Yes." Quinn let the word hang in the air for a moment. She felt a wave of dislike for this woman, an emotion she quickly pushed back down, something she was always telling her patients not to do. She had no intention, though, of making excuses for the size of her office.

"Can I get you anything before we start?" Quinn made sure her voice sounded pleasant.

The woman's eyes darted in Quinn's direction as she ran her fingers through her short blonde hair. "Oh, no, I'm perfectly fine."

"What is it that brings you in today, Sylvia?" Quinn took on her therapist voice and smiled at the woman as she spoke.

"Ah, well, that is the question, isn't it?" Sylvia laughed again in the same artificial way she had a moment ago. "I guess I'm at a crossroads of sorts in my life currently and feel the need for some expert advice."

Was it her imagination, or had her new patient just lifted her eyebrows a little disdainfully at the word "expert?"

"Of course, I'll help you in any way I can, but my job is to guide my patients with figuring out for themselves what is best for them."

Sylvia wasn't able to hide her contempt. "Well, however you choose to word it. I have a problem I need help with, and you come highly recommended." Sylvia sniffed and lifted her head.

"Look, I've been having an affair with a married man, but he would rather not see me anymore, and I just don't know what to do about it." Sylvia took a tissue from her purse and dabbed at her eyes. "I suppose I've shocked you?" She shifted her small, fox-like eyes in Quinn's direction.

Quinn couldn't help laughing. "I've been a therapist for

over twenty years, so believe me, it takes more than an affair to shock me."

The woman seemed to relax a little. She gave a little chuckle and crossed her legs. "So, do you think you can help me or not?"

Quinn felt slightly confused, unsure of what this woman was expecting from her. She decided to start with the obvious. "Why don't you tell me about the affair?"

Sylvia's face seemed to light up at the prospect. "Well, let's see. Where to begin..." Sylvia laughed a girlish laugh. "Of course, I'll use a fictitious name when referring to HIM." She had dramatically emphasized the word him and continued in an almost theatrical tone. "Let's call him Charles, shall we? Ireland is such a small country. I can't risk anyone finding out about us. He would be furious. He has a family, you know." Disdain had crept back into Sylvia's voice. "Why a man of fifty would have children as young as his is beyond me. The oldest is five, and the youngest is two. Can you imagine wanting to start a family in your forties? Of course, his wife is much younger, somewhere in her thirties. He realizes now what a mistake he made." Sylvia sighed with satisfaction.

She then settled into her chair to share all the salacious details of the affair. From what Quinn gathered, Charles was rather dull and selfish. The affair had been entirely on his terms. Now, it seemed he had tired of Sylvia and wanted to end their relationship. He had told her it was out of concern for his family, but Sylvia was having none of it. It sounded to Quinn as though she had become somewhat of a stalker, turning up at places he and his wife were sure to be, even attending a play at one of his children's schools. Sylvia seemed to see nothing wrong with her behavior.

"Don't you think Charles deserves to be made uncomfortable? After all, he said he couldn't live without me a few months ago. I think it's up to me to remind him how much we mean to each other. I've got a few more tricks up my sleeve to make his life miserable, believe me."

Quinn did believe her. As she left the clinic, Quinn felt uneasy. She thought she definitely should learn more about the people she was treating. Maybe one of them genuinely did mean to harm her. She would start tomorrow.

THROUGH SOME CASUAL sleuthing in a few local shops, Quinn discovered that Jozef Abram had been hired as a construction laborer in Castlegibbs, a town about ten miles from Ballyfrannen. The commercial contractor he worked for sent a van to Ballyfrannen daily to pick up the men on his crew. Mostly, they were Polish immigrants like Jozef, and most, including Jozef, had no transportation. A new Tesco was being built on the outskirts of Castlegibbs, and these men supplied the labor. Quinn also learned that Jozef and his family lived in a grim little council house in the least desirable section of Ballyfrannen.

Quinn parked Fiona's car a few doors down from the dilapidated building. She had thought it best to drive Fiona's car rather than her own for obvious reasons. Fiona had been warned against driving the Volvo. Quinn had told her it needed new brakes. She would not endanger Fiona. Quinn wasn't sure what she expected to find, but she thought it was at least a place to start.

After half an hour, a woman of about thirty left the townhouse. She had the hard face of a woman who had never known much joy, already losing whatever attractiveness she possessed in her youth. A small boy of about four walked alongside her as she pushed a tattered-looking pram down the pavement. The pram held a screaming toddler. The woman occasionally reached in, absent-mindedly, to pat the child.

Quinn's heart went out to the little trio. What a life they must lead, with nothing but poverty and a husband and father who came home every evening to take his anger out on them. Quinn resolved to work harder at getting Jozef to manage his anger better. She would ask him to come in twice a week instead of once and step up the inner child work she had already started. None of this was bringing her any closer in finding out who had tried to harm her, though. Tomorrow, she would visit Madeleine Tricot. Colin had told her that Madeleine was staying at the Highgate Hotel in Ballyfrannen. Quinn would call her to see if she would agree to meet.

Quinn sat in the little restaurant area to the side of the lobby of the Highgate Hotel. The Highgate was just the sort of hotel Quinn loved. Decorated in the traditional Irish style, the hotel had warm wood paneling, brass railings, and old, rustic-looking tile floors. Large potted plants filled the tall round tables that stood in several areas within the lobby. The lobby, including the small eating area where Quinn now sat, had comfortable leather chairs and dark wooden tables perfect for tea and sandwiches. It all felt intimate and cozy, with a polished yet worn look that came with age.

Quinn tried to smile as she saw Madeleine exit the small elevator and head towards her. She looked as stylish as ever in a grey silk blouse and grey trousers. Her makeup was skillfully applied, and she wore a pair of small silver hoop earrings that complemented her outfit.

Madeleine approached the table with a look of contempt on her face. "You have come to apologize for your rude behavior, no?" She glared at Quinn belligerently.

Quinn put on her best therapist face and hid her anger at the remark. "I came because I felt we got off on the wrong foot that day at the cottage, and I was hoping we could start again. Shall we order some tea?"

Madeleine sat down across from Quinn and began snapping her fingers at the young woman who had just sat a tray laden with tea and chicken salad sandwiches down at the next table.

Quinn cringed as Bridget Madden's younger sister, Darby, who was also earning money for university, approached their table with a dark look on her face. Quinn, who knew the girl well, smiled apologetically as she ordered tea for herself and Madeleine.

"I'm not sure what you mean about the wrong feet! I am just here because I think you have come to your senses and decided to sell me the land I asked you about."

Madeleine was not one for chitchat, Quinn decided. "No, Fiona and I haven't changed our minds about selling any of our land, but I thought if we were going to be neighbors, we should at least try to be friends."

"How can I be friends with such selfish people? You tell me that? I have told you how much my husband needs his privacy, and still, you won't listen to reason. What do two women your age need with so much land, anyway? I would think you would be happy to be rid of the extra work."

Quinn was finding it hard to control her anger. "You can't seriously expect other people to just put their wishes aside and do whatever you want them to do, can you? Where did you get such a sense of entitlement anyway? Do you think attractive women just have to stamp their feet to get anything they want? I think you'll find that as you get older, that won't continue to work for you. You should try to develop new skills where other people are concerned."

Madeleine looked outraged at Quinn's comments. She jumped up from the table just as Darby Madden arrived with the tea tray. Dishes flew in every direction before landing with a crash onto the hard tile floor.

"Out of my way, you clumsy girl!"

Everyone in the lobby turned to watch Madeleine Tricot march back to the elevator and punch the button repeatedly before folding her arms to wait for the lift.

THAT EVENING, as Quinn sat by the fire pretending to read, hoping Fiona wouldn't see how preoccupied she was, Quinn reviewed the information she had gathered.

Agnes Meek was still at the top of her list since she was the only person Quinn knew who owned a silver car. Agnes could easily blame Quinn, her therapist, for all her problems. This kind of transference was not uncommon. Quinn wondered, not for the first time, how Agnes's sister had died. Had she fallen into the creek and drowned, or had Agnes been responsible for her death? And what was Agnes capable of now? She lived in a more complete state of denial than just about any patient Quinn had ever encountered. Had all those years of denial caused Agnes to become truly deranged?

Quinn couldn't rule out Madeleine Tricot either. She was a person who considered no one's needs but her own. How far would she go to get what she wanted? Quinn couldn't be sure it hadn't been Madeleine's car that had tried to run her off the road. Her light grey Audi might appear silver in the sunlight.

And then there was Jozef Abram. From his temperament, he seemed the most likely to act on his anger, but where would he have gotten a car? There was always the possibility he had stolen one.

Quinn still hadn't done any checking on Thomas Lafferty. She didn't even know whether he owned a car. That should be easy enough to find out, though, with Thomas and Megan living above Timothy McGee's pub.

Quinn felt she wasn't making much progress. She sighed and looked up from her book. Fiona was sitting in the chair across from her with a sour expression on her face.

"I will not be kept in the dark any longer. Tell me what is going on with you and don't say 'nothing' because I know better. You've been looking at the same page in that book for forty-five minutes and acting weird for days. I know something is wrong, so tell me what it is." Fiona crossed her arms and glared at Quinn.

Quinn, feeling she had no choice, told Fiona about the two incidents with the cars and her suspicions that one of her patients might be behind it. She didn't mention any patients by name, feeling that would breach their doctor-patient relationship.

Fiona sat listening with an ever-increasing expression of horror on her face. When Quinn finished, Fiona spoke in an exasperated tone. "Quinn, we're going to the police first thing in the morning. You can't handle something like this by yourself. I know you feel you have to protect your patients, but this is serious."

QUINN AND FIONA sat in the Garda office waiting to see Dermot Brennan. Dermot was the only officer on duty in Ballyfrannen during the day. Other guards worked the night shift, but Quinn wasn't familiar with them. Quinn knew Dermot through his mother. She was a chatty woman, well into middle age, who worked in one of the shops. Quinn knew Sophie Brennan to be a terrible gossip and busybody, and this knowledge made her even less willing to discuss her patients with Dermot. However, she would have no problem telling him about the incidents with Madeleine Tricot.

Dermot sat with a pen and notepad and what looked, to Quinn, to be a bored expression on his face. He was a slightly built man of less than average height. The Garda uniform he wore was at least one size too large. He seemed nervous, constantly bouncing his leg as he waited for Quinn to continue. Quinn recounted the incident of almost being hit by a car in front of Daily Kneads, then being chased and nearly being run off the road on her way into town. When she had finished, Dermot sat with his head down, tapping his pen against the paper as though reviewing his notes. His leg still bounced nervously against the desk. Finally, Dermot raised his head.

"Well now, Missus, you're new to Ireland, aren't ye? Just moved here from the States, am I right?"

"I moved here last April when my friend and I bought the Gillpatrick farm," responded Quinn.

Dermot gave Fiona a quick, dismissive appraisal. "Well, my point is that you're still new to the Irish roads and all. We get plenty of Americans coming in the front door of this office complaining about the driving here in Ireland."

Dermot sniffed and looked a little resentful as he tilted his chair far back and intertwined his hands behind his head. Suddenly, his swivel chair began to tip over backward. Dermot's eyes bulged as he scrambled to right himself.

He suddenly reminded Quinn of Barney Fife from the television series popular in the sixties. She suppressed the urge to laugh. She caught Fiona's eye and realized her friend was thinking the same thing.

Adjusting himself and trying to look like nothing had happened, Dermot smirked then said, "I guess I'll just have to be keepin' my eye out for any menacing-looking silver cars." He seemed quite amused at the thought. "Apart from that, I can't think of much else I can do. You didn't see the driver, you don't know what kind of car it was, and you didn't get a license plate number." Dermot threw his hands up in mock dismay.

"Thank you for your time anyway," responded Quinn as she got up to leave.

Fiona followed suit. Quinn had to give her friend credit for biting her tongue. As the door to the Garda office closed behind them, they both exploded in laughter. They walked down the street towards Daily Kneads, with Fiona doing a mean impression of Dermot Brennan.

After settling in the little cafe and having their tea brought by Bridget, Quinn and Fiona discussed what to do next.

"Didn't you say you still have one patient you haven't done any checking on?" Fiona stirred milk and sugar into her tea.

"Yes, but it shouldn't be hard to find out what kind of car he drives since I know where he lives."

"Quinn, I know you can't say much about your patients, but I feel so helpless. I know so little about any of them. Of course, I wouldn't put this past that little witch, Madeleine Tricot. Boy, I'd like to get ahold of her in a dark alley some-time. I'd show her a thing or two." Fiona sighed, thoroughly enjoying the fantasy.

"I don't know, Fee, maybe I'm overreacting to the whole thing. I'm almost beginning to think they were two separate freak encounters. I can't even say precisely that it was a silver car the first time. Perhaps the roads are just full of careless drivers, like Dermot said."

This sent Fiona into another round of impressions. She took on a serious expression and began bouncing her knee up and down while hunched over the table, pretending to take notes. Then, leaning back in her chair and flailing her arms and legs the way Dermot had to keep from tipping over. This sent them both into renewed gales of laughter, which caused Bridget to stare at them from behind the counter and shake her head.

Quinn sighed, feeling better than she had in a while. "Why don't we just forget the entire thing, Fiona? Nothing else has happened, and I think nothing else will."

"Okay, I guess, but I still want you to check out what kind of car that other patient drives. You said he lives in town, so that shouldn't be a problem. And try to stay alert to anything strange going on; will you do that?" Fiona was getting a worried look on her face again.

"I promise I will find out what kind of car he drives, and I also promise to be alert to anything else that seems off. Now get that look off your face and let's enjoy the rest of the day."

They each took a sip of tea and relaxed a little as they sat looking out the window, finally enjoying the beautiful Irish day.

CHAPTER 14

hree months had passed since Quinn and Fiona had visited Dermot Brennan at the Garda office. Nothing else had happened, and Quinn was feeling her old self. Her worries had receded into the back of her mind. Spring was around the corner, filling Quinn with anticipation at the thought of getting back onto the land. She and Fiona had planned to plant a number of trees around their property and turn some pasture near the cottage into a small vegetable garden. Fiona had started the seedlings for the garden months ago in her greenhouse. Fiona had also given Quinn all the proper names of the trees they would plant and the name of every vegetable seedling she had started for their garden. Quinn, as usual, let it go in one ear and out the other. She enjoyed plants of every kind a great deal but didn't feel the need to learn any of their names.

Quinn and Fiona thought it odd that no construction had started on the land the Tricots had purchased next to their farm. They had expected to see work beginning long before now. Quinn had not asked Colin about it, though, feeling she should respect his work the same way he respected hers.

She and Colin had been seeing each other for several months, but they were taking things slowly. Quinn had to admit her feelings for him had only deepened, and she felt that for the first time, she had got it right when it came to the man in her life. She was glad there was no need to hurry things along, since she was perfectly content with her life exactly the way it was. And how many people could say that?

Quinn was still seeing many of the same patients. Jozef Abram was now deeply involved in dealing with the issues of his childhood. Quinn had taught him how to comfort his inner child when he was feeling scared or angry. She would have him imagine himself as a little boy, the little Jozef who had endured the daily beatings and verbal abuse at the hands of his mother. She had Jozef imagine sitting this little boy on his lap, putting his arm around him, and telling him that he, the adult Jozef, would take care of him now. This helped to ease the self-loathing Jozef and all children of such abuse were left with. Jozef seemed to have gained a more profound understanding of where his angry feelings were coming from. He now knew how deeply his mother had wounded him, not just physically but emotionally. Quinn encouraged him to express his anger towards his mother, knowing that if he did, it would diffuse his anger toward the other women in his life. She felt he had made genuine progress. He no longer sat with his head in his hands, a mass of coiled energy. He was now much more optimistic about his life.

Quinn also discussed the need for Jozef to understand his wife's feelings and empathize with her instead of viewing her as the enemy. She asked him to look at her as a partner and loving companion. These were foreign concepts to Jozef. He had only learned to be unkind and angry with the people in his life. Quinn worked hard to teach him a better way.

They talked about Jozef's children, and what kind of parent Jozef wanted to be. He admitted to being very harsh with his children. Quinn taught him to think of little Jozef and how he would have liked to be treated. This gave him more empathy toward his children. Jozef reported he was enjoying his children much more and felt more deeply bonded with them and his wife. Quinn continually challenged him to build on his successes.

Sylvia Watson continued therapy for a few more months after her first visit. Quinn didn't feel she was making much headway with her. All she wanted to do was discuss the married man she had been seeing and how wonderfully in love they were. Of course, this man had continued to tell her that the affair was over. This seemed to make her more determined to win him back. Nothing Quinn said had any effect. Quinn was beginning to think the woman only came in to have someone to talk to about her exploits. She continued to pursue this man in the most inappropriate ways.

Then, while Quinn and Fiona sat at the kitchen table reading the Irish Times one morning, Quinn saw a familiar face on the newspaper's front page. Sylvia Watson had been arrested. She had broken into the home of a man named Godfrey Owen, the owner of a hardware store in Cork City. The Garda had found a knife in her purse. Quinn felt unsettled and thought again that, as a psychologist, you never really knew whom you were dealing with.

Thomas and Megan had also continued therapy for several more months. Then Megan stopped coming. She didn't feel nervous anymore, she said, and she didn't see any reason to discuss her feelings about losing her father and grandmother. That was ancient history now, she said. Quinn felt that Megan still had a long way to go, but Megan was not the first patient to stop therapy before Quinn would have liked.

Quinn was surprised that Thomas continued therapy

after Megan dropped out. In the past, Quinn had wondered if Thomas might have been coming to therapy out of a need to control Megan and all that she did. Thomas seemed interested in the books Quinn gave him to read, though, starting with The Power of Positive Thinking. After reading that book, he had asked for more. Quinn had given him just about every self-help book she owned, and she encouraged him to watch the Tony Robbins videos that many people, including her, found helpful in changing old patterns.

Thomas had been coming in alone for about a month. He now sat across from Quinn in what was probably the same outfit he had worn on his first visit. His hair was a little shorter now, though, and less unkempt. Quinn thought that Thomas seemed to take a little more pride in how he looked. She wondered if his demeanor was less threatening now, or had she just gotten to know him better?

Thomas sat drumming his fingers on the arm of the chair and rearranging himself frequently as Quinn quietly made a few notes before starting the session.

Noticing Thomas's restlessness, she stopped writing and sat looking at him with a half-smile on her face.

"What? Tell me what's going on, Thomas."

Thomas stopped drumming his fingers and looked at Quinn a little nervously.

"Something's on your mind, so why not just spit it out?" Quinn spoke in the gentle voice she always used with her patients.

Thomas sighed and sat back a little in his chair. "This is hard to say. I mean, I don't want you to think I'm a bad guy or something." Thomas glanced at Quinn, looking a little unsure how to proceed.

"I doubt that I'll think that, Thomas. What's bothering you?"

Thomas still seemed hesitant to speak.

Quinn tilted her head to the side and raised her eyebrows expectantly, waiting to see what Thomas had to say.

Thomas sighed again and gave a little laugh. "Okay, I'll tell you, Dr. Langston. It's about Megan." Thomas ran his fingers through his hair before continuing, as though still reluctant to say what was on his mind.

"I think I'm having second thoughts about getting married. I feel awful about that because I've been saying all this time that I couldn't wait to marry Megan, and that is really the way I felt for a long time. But lately, I've been thinking a lot about what it says in some of the books you gave me."

"What does it say in the books, Thomas?"

"Well, I mean, the parts about figuring out what you want to do with your life and about what kind of relationship you would like to have with the person you marry—you know, stuff like that."

"And have you figured out what you would like to do with your life and what kind of relationship you hope to have with the person you marry?"

"Well, I know I want to avoid driving a truck for the rest of my life." Thomas paused. "I also don't want to be so controlling with the person I marry, and I'm not interested in having that person play mind games with me, either. And I certainly don't want to fight constantly with the person I'm married to."

"Do you feel Megan plays mind games with you?"

Another pause, "Yeah, I think she does."

"Do you and Megan fight often?"

"It feels like we fight all the time." Thomas ran his fingers through his hair again and stood up. "I shouldn't have said anything; I'm probably being disloyal to Megan, talking about her like this." Thomas walked over to the window and looked out.

"Dr. Langston, it's just that those books opened up a whole new world for me, one that I never knew existed, and now I think I want more out of life. Do you know what I mean?"

"I think I know exactly what you mean, Thomas, and I think, right now, you're trying to decide if you deserve more. Am I right?"

"Maybe something like that, I guess." Thomas still kept his face turned toward the window.

"Well, Thomas, all I can say is that you are no less deserving than any other person in this world. Don't you think we all deserve to have the things you're talking about?"

Thomas still stood at the window with his back turned, not answering. Finally, still not turning around, Thomas spoke in a low voice. "I haven't been such a nice guy, Dr. Langston. I've done some things I'm pretty ashamed of."

"Thomas, come back and sit down, will you?"

He did as she asked.

Quinn leaned forward in her chair and gently touched Thomas on the arm. She could see so much emotion written in the stillness of his face. "Thomas, do you consider me to be an honest person?"

Thomas looked at Quinn. "I consider you to be a very honest person, Dr. Langston."

"Then, believe me when I tell you, Thomas, that you are deserving of more, and you have always been. Your dreams are just as important as everyone else's, and you are just as important as everyone else. Thomas, you are such an intelligent man and a kind person. You should find whatever it is in life that makes you happy, and you should do that. And you should decide what kind of relationship you want and with whom, and you should have that, too. Thomas, all people act in ways they are ashamed of. The fact that you feel guilty about your past actions shows how much you've changed. Use that guilt as a reminder of what you don't want to do, and then it will have served a purpose."

Tears slid from Thomas's eyes as he sat with his head down, not speaking. Quinn kept her hand on his arm, and they sat like this for a few moments before Thomas finally spoke.

"Dr. Langston, you don't think it would be wrong of me to break up with Megan?"

"It would be wrong to stay with someone if you don't want to be with them. It would be especially wrong to marry someone you don't genuinely want to marry."

Thomas sat deep in thought for a few more moments.

"Yeah, I think that sounds right. I hope Megan understands when I tell her what I've decided, and … Dr. Langston, I want to apologize for being hard on you in the past. I mean, for a long time, I don't think I gave you much credit. I'm probably not saying this right. What I'm trying to say is, thank you."

QUINN STOOD AT THE WINDOW, watching Thomas walk up the street after their session. As he approached the corner, he crossed to the other side, and Quinn saw him climb into an old, dilapidated silver Toyota.

At that moment, Quinn remembered her promise to Fiona to find out what kind of car Thomas drove. Somehow, she had just never gotten around to it. She knew it was partly because she had felt foolish after her visit with Dermot Brennan. After that, she had just wanted to put the entire episode behind her. Madeleine Tricot had left town, and Quinn felt no further threat. And maybe that was still true. Even if it had been Thomas who had threatened her, didn't he seem changed now? Hadn't he just said he wanted more out of life and was sorry for past wrongs? Quinn decided to say nothing. She felt sure that whatever had happened in the past was better left there. What good would come of dredging it back up?

CHAPTER 15

Spring was in full bloom. Quinn and Fiona were delighted with how the farm was taking shape. They had planted many small trees, dispersing them throughout the land that wasn't laid out in the pasture. They had also tilled the soil for their vegetable garden. Quinn and Fiona cleared away all the overgrown ground cover near the cottage and outbuildings with their new tractor, re-seeded the grass, and planted new beds of shrubs and flowers. They outfitted all the outbuildings, including their barn, with new roofs. The old cottage ruin was now transformed into a small guest house, thanks to Colin. It had a nice-sized sitting room, a small kitchen tucked into one corner, and a lovely, spacious bedroom with a well-appointed full bath. The ceilings were all done in lightly stained wood. They added several skylights to the ceiling in the sitting room to ensure it would be sunny, and they painted the walls a soft green. Natural stone tile was the perfect choice for the floors. They reduced the fireplace size from its original dimensions, and now it was the perfect size for the sitting room. The little cottage had turned out to be as lovely as Quinn and Fiona had hoped. Now, every structure on the property had a well-tended, up-kept look.

Hilda and Tam were both thriving and growing by leaps and bounds. Pike still watched over them and, at times, enjoyed tormenting them by hanging upside down in the little tree that overhung their enclosure. He would then swing back and forth, extending his wings bat-like while making a shrill screech. Hilda and Tam would run around their pen, squealing at the top of their lungs, until Pike grew tired of the game.

The inside of Quinn and Fiona's cottage had a well-lived in look. Quinn's furniture from the States, which for the sitting room consisted of two comfortable wingback chairs and a matching sofa, all with white washable slipcovers, and Quinn's favorite antique pine tables. The coffee table was large and square. It was rustic-looking and perfectly suited the look of the room. Soft-lit lamps, purchased locally, sat on many of the tables. Pictures of farm scenes and animals now hung on the walls. They had found some colorful, easy-care throw rugs for the slate floor. A beautiful antique pine chest that Quinn and Fiona had found in an antique shop and restored now sat near the fireplace. On the opposite wall stood an ancient pine cupboard they had found in the barn and refinished, restoring it to its rightful place in the cottage. Each study held a wooden desk and a comfortable chair, with good lighting nearby for reading. Just as they'd thought, the studies worked well as places to spend time whenever either felt the need for solitude. The arrangement had worked out perfectly for them, and nothing suited them better than spending time at Raven Hill Farm, either working or curling up with a cup of tea.

Life had settled into a series of very pleasant rituals. Their morning chats with Margaret were especially enjoyable. Margaret would show up at their back door, unannounced, once or twice a week, carrying a large bag of Maureen's sweet rolls (or whatever else her mother had baked that morning) and ask if they were ready for a cuppa. The three would arrange themselves comfortably around the kitchen table and sit sipping their tea and enjoying whatever treats Maureen had made for them, idly exchanging the local gossip or being entertained by stories of some of the more colorful guests who had stayed at the O'Callaghan's bed-and-breakfast. Daniel would occasionally join his sister on these morning visits. When he did, he and Fiona would usually end the visit with a walk around the farm, ostensibly for Daniel to see how the pigs were doing, but Margaret and Quinn weren't fooled. They knew how fond Daniel and Fiona were becoming of each other and approved heartily of the situation.

ONE MORNING, when Colin and Quinn were inspecting the new roofs and tuck-pointing on the sheds, Colin mentioned the Tricots. He said he expected Madeleine and Bruno to return to Ballyfrannen the next day. They would complete their plans within the next few days after hitting a snag with the building permission people that had needed to be ironed out. Since there had never been a house on the land they purchased, they required special permission to build it there. Ireland, and especially County Cork, was very strict regarding such matters. Colin felt that in this case, though, they would make an exception since the Tricots were such a famous couple and would most certainly be an asset to the local area, which was always seeking an edge when attracting tourists. Quinn tried to hide her disappointment at the news and wondered again how Colin could have such a radically different opinion of Madeleine Tricot than she had.

After Colin left, Quinn headed to the greenhouse. She

dreaded giving Fiona the news regarding the Tricots, but she knew it had to be done. Fiona was always at her best when spending time with her plants, so Quinn felt it would be the safest place to tell her the news.

Fiona stood with her back to Quinn, humming some tune Quinn didn't recognize. Quinn watched as she gently pulled a large fern from the pot it had overgrown and placed it expertly into a larger one, gently tapping the soil down around the roots.

"There you go; that should feel better." Fiona always talked to her plants in a gentle voice that she seldom used otherwise.

She sounded so happy; Quinn had a moment's guilt at spoiling her pleasure. It had to be done, though, and better she hear it from her than to find Madeleine Tricot at their door again on some odious mission to bend them to her will.

"Fiona, do you have a moment?"

"Sure, Quinnie, what's up?" Fiona, who hadn't turned around, still had a lightness in her voice that those who knew her seldom heard.

"Colin was here today; he mentioned the Tricots will return tomorrow. He thinks they can get building permission now and should be able to start work on their home soon." Quinn waited for the explosion she knew would come.

Fiona's expression morphed. She now had a thunderous look in her eyes. She pulled off her gardening gloves and threw them down beside the newly repotted fern. "Oh, good grief, just when everything was going so well. Quinn, if that woman starts up again with us, I'll run her down with my car!" Fiona paused momentarily and looked at Quinn with an expression acknowledging her poor choice of words before proceeding with her tirade. "Really, Quinn, what is Colin thinking, building a house for a woman like that?

You'd think out of loyalty to us, or at least to you, he would tell that little narcissist to take a hike."

"I'm as disappointed as you are, Fee, but I guess they have a right to build a house there if they want. I don't think they will bother us anymore. In the end, things will work out, I'm sure.

"Quinn, for a psychologist, you certainly are naïve. Those people could quite possibly make our lives a living hell. Why don't you ask Colin to sever all contact with them?"

"Fiona, you know I can't do that, and, anyway, they would just find another builder to build their house for them."

"Well, I suppose you've got a point, but it makes me sick to think of those people living next door."

Quinn and Fiona left the greenhouse together, feeling quite miserable.

The news that the Tricots would soon be their neighbors still preoccupied Quinn the next day. She hated to admit it, but she did feel a little resentful towards Colin for working with the couple. He seemed so enamored of their fame and oblivious to the kind of person Madeleine really was.

CHAPTER 16

*Q*uinn was lost in thought when she realized Agnes Meek was standing at the door of her office.

"Dr. Langston, my sessions should have started five minutes ago. I haven't got all day to sit out there in that horrible waiting room, cooling my heels."

Agnes, who was heavily made up as usual and smelled like she had used an entire bottle of expensive perfume, caught Quinn's attention.

"I'm sorry, Agnes. I lost track of the time. Why don't you come in and have a seat? Don't worry about the time; I can make it up at the end of the session."

Agnes seemed somewhat appeased as she sat down, dropping another expensive handbag onto the carpet.

"Now, Agnes, why don't you tell me what kind of week you've had?" began Quinn.

"It's been alright, I guess. I've been doing a lot of thinking about my sister lately, though. That makes me uncomfortable, and every so often, I even have bad dreams about her."

"Could you tell me about the dreams?" asked Quinn.

"They're bad dreams. I've already told you that."

Agnes always takes things so literally, thought Quinn.

"Could you describe one of those bad dreams about your sister?"

"Do I have to? I told you they make me uncomfortable."

Agnes hasn't lost any of her childish behavior, thought Quinn.

"I wouldn't ask you if I didn't feel it would be helpful to your progress."

"There hasn't been any progress if you ask me, but I can tell you about one of my dreams, I guess." Agnes sighed to let Quinn know she wasn't pleased. "Sometimes, I'm with my sister, standing by the stream. And then, all of a sudden, I notice my sister is in the stream, and she looks up at me and says, 'Why don't you save me, Agnes?'"

Agnes distractedly picked up her purse as she spoke and rummaged through its contents, seemingly intent on finding something.

"Agnes, could you not do that right now?"

"Not do what?" Agnes stared at her vacantly.

"Not rummage through your purse."

"Why not?"

"Well, sometimes you use your purse, or something else, as a distraction to keep from feeling an unpleasant emotion, like just now when you were talking about the dream and your sister asking you why you didn't save her. That brought up some emotion you would rather not deal with, so you distracted yourself with your purse. It's a common enough response; we all distract ourselves from emotions we would rather not deal with. Only sometimes, we do have to stop and deal with them. That's what I want you to do right now, Agnes. I want you to tell me how you feel in the dream when your sister asks you why you don't save her. Can you tell me?"

Agnes reluctantly sat her purse back down on the carpet

and looked at Quinn. "I feel frozen in the dream, like a block of ice or something. What I'm saying is that I don't feel anything ... nothing. I think that's the part that makes me the most uncomfortable. I should feel something, shouldn't I? That's unnatural, isn't it?"

Agnes got a worried look on her face and reached down for her purse, then stopped herself and sat back in her chair. "Does this mean I'm crazy? It doesn't seem right that I felt nothing in that dream, does it?"

Quinn smiled reassuringly at Agnes. You can't access your feelings yet, that's all. That's why you're here, so that we can change that."

Agnes' mood suddenly changed. She had that look on her face that was quite familiar to Quinn, one that reminded her of a petulant child. "Well, I've been coming here for months and months, so why hasn't it helped already?"

Quinn tried to hide a feeling of annoyance. "It takes time, Agnes. You've got years of repressed feelings to overcome. It won't happen overnight, but you've already made progress. When you started coming, you told me repeatedly that your childhood was great and that you never thought about your sister anymore."

"Well, that was a lie. I think about her; I've had that same dream since I was a little girl. Since she died, I think." Agnes looked like she was about to cry.

"And you do feel something, Agnes. You wouldn't look like that if you didn't."

An open, genuine smile spread across Agnes's face as she looked up at Quinn. "Do you really think that, Dr. Langston?"

Then, as though Agnes had forgotten herself for a moment, she abruptly stopped smiling and complained again about how long Quinn had kept her waiting.

Oh, well, thought Quinn, a little progress was better than none.

After her next appointment, Quinn left the clinic for lunch with one of the other therapists. Nola Baird was a pleasant woman. Quinn guessed her to be in her mid-thirties. She had three small children, twin four-year-old boys and a two-year-old little girl. Like Quinn, Nola worked part time at the clinic. Quinn felt they even looked somewhat alike. Nola was petite, like her, and wore her dark hair in the same short style as Quinn's. Several patients at the clinic had asked if they were sisters. Quinn didn't know Nola well, so she looked forward to the lunch as a way of becoming better acquainted. They decided to eat at one of the local pubs.

Gus Toner's Pub was already full of patrons when Quinn and Nola settled into one of the small tables near the front. Quinn didn't usually eat a big meal at lunchtime, but the carvery had looked so delicious she had joined Nola in ordering a big plate of roasted pork with carrots, turnips, and potatoes.

They were just tucking into their food when Quinn noticed Colin sitting at a table near the back. She stood up and began walking towards him to say hello before realizing he was not alone. She stopped and stood motionless in the noisy pub as she watched Colin, who was unaware of her presence. He sat at a small table, conversing intimately with a woman. Their heads were close together. Colin had just reached over and touched the woman's arm. She looked up at him and smiled at something he said.

Then Colin noticed Quinn standing on the other side of the pub, and the color seemed to drain from his face. He rose as though to go to her, but Quinn was faster. She headed back to her table, grabbed her bag, and, with a quick word to Nola, ran out of the pub. Her heart pounded uncomfortably, and she heard a funny ringing in her ears as she headed toward her car. She could still see the face of Madeleine Tricot smiling up at Colin in the pub.

Quinn climbed into her Volvo and drove off as fast as she could, headed for home and the comfort of Fiona and the cottage. Tears were burning her eyes and making it hard to see. The humiliation she felt each time she replayed the scene in her head had a smothering quality. Quinn struggled to catch her breath. Would she ever learn when it came to men?

By the time Quinn reached the cottage, she had composed herself somewhat. She could hear Fiona trying to open the door from the other side as she turned the key in the lock.

"I thought I heard your car in the lane." Fiona smiled as she pulled the door open. "Quinn, you'll never guess who stopped by this morning! Oh, don't even bother trying to guess; you could never. Well, go ahead and guess anyway."

Quinn was glad for the momentary distraction. "Graham Norton?"

"Oh, don't be ridiculous," said Fiona laughingly. "It was somebody famous, though."

"Why don't you just tell me who it was, Fiona?"

"Okay, I will. It was Bruno Tricot. Can you believe it?"

Quinn felt the need to sit down, so she pushed past her friend and headed for one of the wing chairs in the sitting room. Once seated, Quinn sighed heavily and answered her friend, "No, I can't believe it, to tell you the truth. What did he want, our firstborn and the deed to our farm?"

"Quinn, don't be silly! I know you won't believe this, but I really liked him. He isn't like his wife or a famous person. He was kind, soft-spoken, and thoughtful, and he is a gardener, too. We talked about plants for hours. He knows the name of every plant in my greenhouse; can you believe that?"

"This day is getting more unbelievable by the moment,"

answered Quinn in a voice that shook slightly. Quinn could feel tears beginning to slide down her cheeks.

Finally, Fiona noticed her friend's distress. "Quinn, what on earth has happened?"

Fiona sat down opposite Quinn's chair and said in a soft voice, "Quinnie, tell me what's happened."

Quinn tumbled over the words as she told Fiona about seeing Colin with Madeleine Tricot in the pub. When she had finished, Fiona's reaction was not what she had expected.

"Are you sure they were up to no good, Quinn? Maybe you misinterpreted the situation, don't you think that's possible?"

"I don't think so, Fee. They looked awfully chummy, and the look on his face when he saw me—I mean, he looked so guilty. Why would he look like that if nothing were going on?"

"I don't know, Quinn. It just sounds so unlike Colin. Has he tried to call you?"

"Yes, but I turned my phone off on the way home. I would rather not talk to him. I know he will make it all sound harmless, but it didn't look that way to me, and I don't want to be hurt like that again. Unfortunately, I care about him so much he has the power to really level me. I don't like that. I don't want anyone to have that much power over me ever again. Men have hurt me too many times.

Fiona was silent for a long moment and then looked sternly at her friend. "Quinn, that's the coward's way out."

"Maybe you're right, Fee, but I don't care. I don't want to love anyone so much they can destroy me like that."

Fiona knew reasoning with her was useless. She rose from her chair and laid a hand on Quinn's shoulder. "I'll fix us some coffee and sandwiches. You haven't had lunch yet, have you?"

Quinn shook her head no as her mind, once again, replayed the scene in the pub.

Quinn woke the next morning, still resolute in her desire to have nothing more to do with Colin. She had relived the events in the pub all night, and still, she couldn't believe what she had seen had been harmless. Maybe Fiona was right when she said she was taking the coward's way out, but she wasn't willing to expose herself like that anymore—not with men, anyway. Maybe she was just too old for love.

None of this was making Quinn feel any better. She finally dragged herself out of bed and into the shower, deciding that a long walk around the farm was what she needed right now.

Quinn breathed in the fresh air as she walked into the Irish countryside. Spring was Quinn's favorite time of year in Ireland. There was rain in the air, but it hadn't come yet, just the soft dampness that precedes it.

She paused to admire the gently rolling hills. To say they were green didn't really do them justice. There were so many varying shades of that color in every direction. Then gorse's golden blooms blanketed the hedgerows, creating a delightful patchwork. Quinn could smell its light scent, which reminded her of coconuts. Maggie, who was always happy to be outside, ran ahead of her, barking and then circling back to walk at her heels for a few moments before running off again in another direction. Pike sat perched on Quinn's shoulder, emitting a soft, gurgling croak into her ear that he used in his most gentle moments. Both Maggie and Pike sensed Quinn's sadness, and both were trying their best to cheer her up. Her eyes welled up with gratitude for the kinship she felt toward these two creatures.

Just as Quinn felt a little more herself, she noticed a truck, and a car parked in the lane in front of the land next to her farm. With a jolt, she realized the truck was Colin's. She could make him out in the distance as he walked along, pointing now and then at something on the Tricots' land. With a sickening lurch of her stomach, Quinn realized that the woman walking at his side was Madeleine Tricot. She could see her stop and turn occasionally to look up at Colin. They looked like a happy couple out for a stroll.

Quinn quickly turned towards the cottage, calling Maggie to do the same. She walked the rest of the way home without looking back, her heart hardening towards Colin with every step.

CHAPTER 17

*Q*uinn decided she would ask Fiona about Bruno Tricot's visit yesterday. She had been so upset when Fiona had told her about him she could remember very little of what her friend had said. Quinn had already decided she wouldn't mention anything more about Colin to Fiona. She wanted to drop the subject permanently, but she was still interested in finding out what the Tricots intended to do with their land.

Quinn adjusted her expression into what she hoped was a pleasant one as she walked through the back door. Fiona sat at the kitchen table with a big plate of eggs and sausages in front of her. She had just taken a large bite of sausage, dripping with egg yolk. Quinn sat down across from her and poured herself a cup of tea, stirring in milk and sugar before speaking.

"Fiona, I know you told me about your visit with Bruno Tricot when I got home yesterday, but I was so upset I really can't remember much of what you said. I wondered if you would mind telling me again?"

"Sure, Quinn," Fiona chewed the remains of the massive

mouthful of food and then rubbed at her mouth with a napkin before continuing. "Bruno stopped by right after you left for work yesterday. I was in the greenhouse doing some repotting, and he pecked on the glass and then came in and introduced himself. You can imagine how amazed I was at how nice he seemed. I can't understand why he ever married someone like Madeleine. He seems like a gentle soul who enjoys puttering around in a garden as much as I do. He complimented us on how nice the farm looked and said he hoped his house would look half as nice when it was built. Really, the man seemed to have no ego. He never even mentioned being famous, or making films, or anything like that. I think you would like him, Quinn."

"And he didn't say anything about wanting to buy some of our land?"

"No, nothing like that ... well, wait, now that you mention it, he did say something in passing about wondering if we would consider selling him our guest house and a small amount of land. He said it so matter-of-factly that I didn't even think about it again until you asked just now."

"What did you say when he asked about buying the guest house?"

"I said I didn't have a problem with it but would have to talk to you first. That doesn't sound like me, does it?" Fiona furrowed her brow and pulled at her lower lip. "Gee, it's almost like he cast a spell over me or something. It's just that the man is so likable, and we seemed to have so much in common. I was excited that he would be my neighbor." Fiona chuckled and sighed, "I don't know what to tell you, Quinn; the man is a fifty-five-year-old Don Juan. No wonder Madeleine, the model, fell for him."

. . .

QUINN SAT in her office the next day, making notes at her desk for her next session. She wasn't expecting any patients for over an hour.

Quinn heard a light tap and realized Nola Baird had stuck her head around the corner of her door. "Quinn, there's a Bruno Tricot here to see you." Nola made a face and shrugged in response to the questioning look on Quinn's face. "Do you want me to send him in?"

Quinn sat thinking for a moment before responding. "Thanks, Nola. Please ask him to come in."

Bruno Tricot walked through the doorway of Quinn's office. He was quite tall and thin, except for a slight paunch around the middle. His thinning hair had turned grey. He had an ashen look to his face, and he also looked terribly out of shape. There was nothing attractive about him. His only redeeming quality was the keen intelligence so evident in his eyes. For a moment, Quinn got an amusing mental image of Bruno and the illustrious Madeleine in the throes of passion. Then she thought of Colin and Madeleine, so intimate in the pub yesterday, and all her amusing thoughts vanished.

"Mr. Tricot, what can I do for you?" Quinn stood and stretched out her hand towards her visitor.

"Madame, it is truly a pleasure finally to make your acquaintance."

Bruno hurried towards Quinn's outstretched hand and kissed it before smiling down at her. "I hope you will pardon my indiscretion. I know this is not the proper way to greet a beautiful woman here in Ireland."

Oh, good God, thought Quinn, as she motioned for Bruno to have a seat.

"Is there something I can do for you, Mr. Tricot?" Quinn was hoping to get this visit over with as quickly as possible.

"Please, call me Bruno. You are a psychologist, is that not so?"

"Yes, that's right, um, Bruno."

"It is a field I, myself, once thought of going into."

"Is that so?" Quinn kept her face expressionless and her voice flat. "I thought your interests were films and gardening?"

Bruno looked at Quinn carefully before speaking."Ah, you are correct, Madam. I have a great interest in those things, but I am also quite interested in how people think, as are you; that is why you became a psychologist, is that not right?" Bruno looked at her intently.

Quinn felt like a mouse being stared at by a cat. "I suppose that is true enough, but I'm sure you didn't come here to discuss how I chose my career." Quinn smiled just enough to temper her words slightly.

Bruno looked at Quinn sharply before continuing. "You are right, Madam; that is not why I am here. I can see you are a busy woman, so I will tell you why I have come to see you today. Maybe your dear friend told you that I visited your farm the day before yesterday? I hoped to catch both of you at home, but you had already left for work, so I spoke with Fiona. I believe, from our conversation, that she has already told you a little of my reason for stopping by your farm."

Quinn had a pretty good idea where this was going, but she didn't intend to make this any easier for Madeleine Tricot's husband. "She told me you had a passion for gardening and that you and she spent a great deal of time discussing the plants in her greenhouse."

"This is true, of course. We did speak of gardening." Bruno did his best to hide his annoyance. "Fiona, also, might have mentioned my desire to purchase a small amount of your property, no? I am aware my wife approached you with an offer to purchase ten acres of your land some time ago. She has told me you have no interest in selling off such a large portion of your farm, but I thought you might be willing to part with your small guest house if I offered you, say, three hundred and fifty thousand euros for it?"

"That would be a great deal of money for such a little guest house. May I ask why you and your wife have so much interest in purchasing part of our property?"

"Well, I always believe it is best to speak honestly, so I will tell you." Bruno seemed relieved to finally be able to get to the point of his visit.

"My wife, she is the one who found this property next to your farm. She fell in love with its beautiful green hills, which, as you know, stretch down to the sea. She purchased the property the very day she saw it. She did not bother to consult me before doing so, and she did not bother to inquire whether the land could be built upon." Bruno scowled and then sighed resignedly before continuing. "She is a woman who is used to getting what she wants. Later, we discovered we could not build on this property, even though we had paid a small fortune for it. There has never been a dwelling on that land, so the building permission board will not allow a house to be built there. We asked that they make an exception in this case since my wife and I are both very famous people. This was our builder's idea. He thought they might feel we would be an asset to the area." Bruno threw up his hands and rolled his eyes as though embarrassed to be saying such a thing. "But, we were told yesterday that they have turned us down again. So, now, here we sit with this expensive land but no way to build on it. The building permission board has said they will only allow us to do so if we purchase the adjoining land that already has a dwelling on it. Since your guest house was once a farmer's cottage, owning that and a small amount of land surrounding it would allow us to obtain building permission."

Bruno sat back in his chair before continuing.

"Do you follow what I am saying, dear lady?" Bruno

smiled, what was undoubtedly his most charming smile. "I have a feeling my wife was quite rude when she approached you regarding our situation, but I am here to make amends in the hope that we can reach an agreement. What do you say, Dr. Langston? Shall we start again as friends and come to an agreement regarding your little guest house?" Bruno smiled at Quinn again, seemingly confident of her answer.

Quinn sat for a moment before speaking, choosing her words carefully.

"Mr. Tricot...Bruno, I must tell you that I have no interest in selling our guest house. It sits quite close to our cottage, as you know, and selling it is not something I would ever consider doing. I'm afraid Fiona now feels the same. I sympathize with your situation, but there isn't anything I can do to help you." Quinn had kept her face expressionless, but her voice had been stern.

Quinn watched the smile fade from Bruno Tricot's face. It was replaced with a look of pure hatred.

"I think you will live to regret this decision, Madam."

"Is that a threat?" Quinn felt a quick release of adrenaline and sat forward in her chair. Her eyes narrowed, and she spoke in a low voice, "You have no idea how much I hate bullies, Mr. Tricot." Quinn struggled to reign in her anger. She took a deep breath before continuing, "Now, I think you had better get out of my office, and be warned, I will not tolerate any further threats from either you or your wife."

Bruno Tricot rose quickly from the chair and, with a parting glare over his shoulder, quietly left her office.

Quinn attempted to regain her composure. Again, she couldn't help wondering how Colin could have such high regard for the French couple. Why could he not see them for who they really were? She couldn't remember meeting two more disagreeable people. Well, maybe his eyes were clouded by his attraction to Madeleine. Quinn felt anger rising again.

Just then, she realized that Nola was, again, at her door.

"Quinn, are you okay? Your door was open, so I could hear most of what was said. That man has a nerve talking to you like that! Would you like a cup of tea? You still have a few minutes before your next patient arrives."

Quinn tried to smile, still unable to thoroughly shake off her anger. "Tea would be nice, Nola. Would you care to join me in a cup? I could use the distraction to clear my head."

After Quinn and Nola were settled with their tea, Nola said, "Quinn, It is not my intention to upset you all over again, but I thought I should tell you that Colin spoke to me for a bit after you ran out of... I mean, after you left the pub the other day. I know Colin fairly well. He's done some work for my husband and me. Before the twins were born, we added on another bedroom, and Colin was our contractor." Nola looked unsure whether she should continue. "I just don't want you to think I'm keeping something from you. I know you and Colin have been seeing each other, even though we have never spoken about it."

Nola waited to see if Quinn was going to say anything. When she didn't, Nola continued.

"Quinn, I know we don't know each other very well, but I do consider you a friend." Nola hesitated again, seeming to gauge the effect her words were having on Quinn. "I thought about this last night, and I would want someone to tell me this if I were in your shoes."

"I'm trying to say that you might have misinterpreted the situation at lunch the other day. I think Colin's only interest in that woman is as a client. I don't believe Colin is the type of man who would behave in a dishonorable manner towards you. I have seen you and Colin together, and I'll have to tell you that what the two of you have is something that doesn't come along every day. Some people settle for a lot less."

Nola stared into space just long enough for Quinn to realize that Nola was thinking about her own marriage.

"I know you are a trained psychologist, but you must know, as well as I do, that it isn't as easy to evaluate your own emotions and what might be at the root of them."

Quinn tried to smile, even though she was feeling increasingly uncomfortable by the minute. "Nola, you think I reacted the way I did because of something in my past?"

"If you've been hurt by a man in the past, you're more likely to tar all men with the same brush." Nola laughed, "I guess I don't sound much like a psychologist, do I? Maybe I'm just speaking as another woman who understands what some men are like. It might be possible that you are judging Colin by the actions of others because of past hurts; you might even be afraid to see Colin for who he really is."

"Okay, now you are sounding like a psychologist." Quinn smiled at Nola, and they both laughed. Quinn continued, "I do see what you mean, and I certainly have more than my share of baggage in that department." Quinn paused for a moment and then added, "I think I need to take some time to sort this out. Thanks, Nola. I know you are trying to help, and I appreciate that. You have given me a fresh perspective, and I will consider what you've said."

With that, the two parted, and Quinn readied herself for her patient.

JOZEF ABRAM HAD MISSED his last two appointments, so Quinn started with that. "I missed you last week, Jozef. Were you ill?"

"If you call being in jail ill, then yes, I was ill." Jozef was back to sitting with his head in his hands.

"Why were you in jail, Jozef?"

"I was in jail because of my mother-in-law! My wife's

mother came for a visit, and all my efforts go right down the drain! There is no pleasing that old woman. She criticizes everything I do. Finally, I have enough, and I explode, and I smash some furniture in my house! And she calls the Garda and tells them I am threatening her, and they take me to jail. I have no money for bail, so I have to spend the whole week there and miss work. This is all horrible for me. What if I lose my job? What then? Now my wife is talking about moving back to Poland to live with her mother. So, I am right back to where I started. This is all your fault!" Jozef stood and pointed his finger in Quinn's face. "You said you would help me, but I am worse off than before."

CHAPTER 18

*Q*uinn drove down the quiet country roads heading
for home. Her upper back ached with tension as she
mentally reviewed the morning's events. Why did
upsets always seem to come in multiples? Wasn't the visit
from Bruno Tricot, the uncomfortable conversation with
Nola, or the meltdown of Jozef bad enough by themselves
without all of them happening one after another? Quinn
realized that most such events were just a part of life, but she
was also beginning to feel that something else was going on,
some shift in her life that she was only now aware of. There
was a little voice at the back of her mind that kept telling her
to be careful, to be watchful. Quinn clutched the steering
wheel and nervously looked into the rearview mirror as she
drove down the narrow road toward home.

As she approached the cottage, Quinn saw Colin's truck
parked in the drive. The tension in her back was now turning
into a pounding headache. She longed to be curled up in the
comfortable chair in her den, with a cup of tea and a book,
and only Maggie and Pike for company. She pulled into the
lane leading to the cottage and parked her Volvo next to

Colin's truck. Reluctantly, she climbed out and headed for the front door.

Colin and Fiona both fell silent as she entered the sitting room. Fiona had an uncomfortable look on her face. Great, thought Quinn. It's nice to know you're being talked about.

Fiona was the first to speak. "Colin just stopped in for a little chat, Quinn. There's tea made if you want some. Is everything alright? You look done in."

Quinn struggled with her emotions as she tried to smile. She battled the urge to cry, desperately wishing to sit beside Colin and confess to him and Fiona how awful her day had been and how scared and vulnerable she was right then.

Suddenly, other thoughts kicked in. Only weak people burdened others like that. The urge to cry receded as the desire to appear in control supplanted her feelings. Only a tiny part of her registered the irony in what she had just done.

Quinn smiled with more confidence now. "I'm fine, Fiona, just a little headache. I would have some tea if you have plenty."

Quinn turned to look at Colin, who was seated on the sofa. "Colin, it's nice to see you." Then she walked towards the hallway. "I'll just be a minute. Pour me a cup of tea, would you, Fee?"

Quinn walked down the hallway and into her bedroom, shutting the door behind her. She leaned against the door for a few moments, eyes closed, forcing down the last of her emotions. Then, after a brief look in the mirror to ensure her face held no residual tension, she opened the door and walked back down the short hallway. By the time she reached the doorway to the sitting room, she was fully in charge of herself again.

Fiona looked up from her chair by the fire. The look on her face indicated she wasn't fooled. Then she gave Quinn an encouraging little wink and motioned towards the coffee table.

"Here's your tea, Quinn. Colin was just giving me a report on the Tricots. It seems that buying our guest house was their last hope for gaining building permission. He said they both spent an hour in his office just now, yelling at him as though the whole thing was his fault."

"Well, it's been my experience that those two have to find someone else to blame apart from themselves. Madeleine should not have purchased the land in the first place without knowing whether she could build on it. Now, they seem to think it's our job to bail them out of their situation. Bruno Tricot paid me a very unpleasant visit this morning. I ended up ordering him out of my office. Frankly, I'm sick of both of them. Our land is not for sale, and neither is our guest house."

Quinn gave Colin a sharp look, almost challenging him to take issue with what she had just said. Then she added, "I guess you have finally gotten a taste of what Fiona and I have been experiencing all along with that couple."

Fiona cleared her throat and then spoke. "I think Bruno could be decent enough if he stopped listening to his wife." Fiona refused to acknowledge Quinn's look in her direction. "I agree with Quinn about Madeleine, though; she really is odious."

Colin sat watching the interaction between Fiona and Quinn. "Frankly, I think you're both saints for having put up with them … and me for that matter."

Then he added more seriously, "Quinn, I think I owe you an apology for not realizing sooner how upsetting my association with Madeleine has been for you. I want you to know that my relationship with that woman was strictly a business one. Madeleine Tricot holds no attraction for me." He looked at Quinn with more than a little tenderness in his eyes. "Any closeness you saw between us in the pub was due to my hearing not being what it used to be and nothing else. I felt horrible when I saw the look on your face." Colin paused for a moment. "I spoke with Nola Baird after you left. I guess I felt the need to explain myself to someone."

Quinn felt strangely unmoved by Colin's words. "Nola mentioned that you had talked to her. We spoke about it today. Now, Colin, I will excuse myself if you don't mind. I've got a pounding headache, and I think I'll lie down for a little while before dinner." With that, Quinn rose and left the room.

Fiona and Colin exchanged subdued glances, and then Colin rose to leave.

"Just give her a little time, Colin," said Fiona. "Quinn has a way to go before she can fully trust someone with her heart again."

Colin nodded in understanding before heading out the door.

"Crap," mumbled Fiona to herself as she gathered the dishes.

Quinn woke up and looked at her watch. She had slept for over two hours. Her headache was gone, though, and her body no longer felt tense. She could smell a pot roast in the oven. Fiona had started supper; she realized with gratitude, even though it was her turn to cook. Quinn climbed out of bed and wandered into the kitchen, still yawning from her nap. She felt a little sheepish for having been so hard on her friend earlier.

"Hi, Fee. Something sure smells good."

"It won't be ready for another hour. Do you need a little something to tide you over? Margaret brought scones this morning, and there's one or two left. They're blueberry ... your favorite."

Quinn sat down at the kitchen table. Fiona's kind words

had their effect. All the emotions she had so successfully suppressed earlier began once again to take her over.

When Quinn didn't answer, Fiona turned around to see her friend sitting with her elbows on the table and her head in her hands.

"Quinnie?" Fiona walked over and put her arm around her. "Do you want to talk or just cry?"

"Just cry." Quinn's head sank further as she sobbed in earnest.

Fiona brought over a scone, a glass of milk, and a box of tissues, placing them in front of Quinn before sitting down and again putting her arm around her friend. They sat like this for some minutes. Finally, Quinn sighed and blew her nose into a tissue. She then reached for the milk and took a long drink before setting the glass back down. She sighed before picking up the scone and nibbling on it. Realizing how hungry she was, she devoured the rest.

"Fee, have I told you lately how glad I am to have you as my friend?"

"Yes, but it's always good to hear it again." Fiona got up from the table and gathered the dishes. "Do you want anything else?"

"No, I'd rather not spoil my appetite. The roast smells delicious."

"It's local beef." Fiona had adopted the Irish habit of asking the butcher where the meat she purchased came from.

"Martin Bray was working yesterday. He always gives me the best cuts. He said that the cow had been raised within ten miles of here. You should have seen how it draped down my arm when I put it in the pan. Meat in the States is usually as stiff as a board."

Quinn started to laugh. "Fiona, you're the only person I know who can speak that lovingly about a pot roast."

Quinn laughed harder, and Fiona, who at first had looked

offended, began to laugh, too. Then, the laughter took on a life of its own, and they laughed until they were both wheezing and crying. Finally, Quinn mopped at her eyes with another tissue and said, "I feel better than I have in days." She gave Fiona a grateful smile.

CHAPTER 19

Quinn felt her life had settled into a comfortable routine. She loved being in Ireland and owning the farm. She took pride in the way she and Fiona had restored the property. The only thing left was what to do with the little guesthouse. It seemed a shame to let the beautiful little structure remain empty. Filling it with old friends visiting from the States didn't really appeal to them. Liam Madden had mentioned using it as a holiday cottage, but that wasn't the answer either.

They decided to discuss their dilemma over what to do with the guest house with Margaret the next time she stopped in for tea. Margaret had a good head for figuring things out, and they valued her opinion.

Margaret knocked on their back door the next morning with her usual bagful of goodies.

"Margaret, you must be psychic; you're just the person we wanted to talk to," said Quinn as she opened the door wider to accommodate Margaret's ample figure.

Margaret tossed the bag onto the kitchen table and helped herself to a cup of tea. Then she grabbed several small plates from the cupboard and placed them on the table as they all sat down to enjoy the sweets and some relaxing conversation.

Fiona spoke through a large mouthful of a cinnamon bun. "Margaret, we can't decide what to do with the guest house. It seems a shame to leave it empty, but we can't come up with a use for it. We don't like the idea of a holiday let, and if friends visit from the States, we would rather they stay in the house with us. But, as I said, we feel guilty about just letting the little house sit empty."

Margaret looked at the ceiling the way she always did when she was thinking. "You know, I might have just the right solution. Do you remember me mentioning Hattie Biggs from Bristol? She's an older lady who stays with us occasionally."

"No," said Fiona, "I don't remember you mentioning anyone by that name."

"Well, that's funny. I was sure I had mentioned Hattie before. She's been coming to Ballyfrannen for a couple of weeks every six months for years. She's quite tall and, well, rather plain, but she's a good, kind woman. I believe she's in her early fifties.

Hattie just retired from her job as an investigator at a detective agency in Bristol. She feels connected to this part of Cork because her mother was born here. Her mother moved away when she got married. Hattie has always said that when she retires, she will move here permanently. Now, she's here searching for a place to live. She never married, so it's just her and her dog. Wolfie is his name; she brings him with her whenever she visits. He's a love. He would get on well with Maggie, I'm sure."

Quinn and Fiona were speechless.

Finally, Fiona spoke. "You're kidding about the detective agency part, aren't you, Margaret?"

Quinn put down her tea and smiled, "I think she made the whole thing up; that person sounds straight out of central casting."

Margaret looked offended. "I most certainly did not invent Hattie Biggs. She is a real person, and she did retire from a detective agency in Bristol, and she is here searching for a place to live. I can't think why ye would say such a thing." Margaret sat her cup down hard, sniffed, and looked out the window.

Realizing they had offended their friend, Quinn was quick to make amends. "I'm sorry, Margaret. I thought you were joking. We would happily meet Hattie Biggs and see if she would be right for the guest house." Quinn glanced at Fiona, who, for once, was being sensitive. She eagerly nodded her head in agreement.

CHAPTER 20

The next day, Quinn and Fiona waited for the arrival of Hattie Biggs. They had no idea what to expect from this meeting. Margaret's description of the overly tall, newly retired detective from Bristol, England, still seemed rather humorous. They were both in a giggly sort of mood and somewhat nervous. Quinn couldn't help giving Fiona one last admonishment as the doorbell rang.

"Don't you dare do anything to embarrass me! Remember, this woman is a friend of Margaret's." Quinn put on her best smile and opened the door.

As the door swung open, Quinn realized she was staring into the chest of a very tall woman indeed. Margaret hadn't been kidding when she said Hattie was tall. She was at least six feet in height. Quinn, who was barely five feet three, had to crane her neck upwards to see the woman's face. It was a long face with prominent features; even her teeth seemed extra large. Her grey hair was pulled back rather severely, and she didn't seem to be wearing any makeup. As Margaret had said, she looked to be in her early fifties. She wore a plain white blouse, a brown jumper, and dark tweed trousers. Her large feet were encased in flat, no-nonsense, brown leather shoes. Quinn had just registered how unattractive this woman was when, suddenly, Hattie's face widened into the most pleasant smile. Mid thought, Quinn had to re-evaluate her initial opinion. Her smile transformed her features into something quite pleasing. The woman stuck out her hand, and Quinn reached up to shake it.

"Hello, I'm Hattie Biggs. Margaret said I should stop by this afternoon to look at your guest house. She said you were thinking of renting it. I hope you were expecting me?"

Quinn realized she was still staring at the woman's face. She found it striking in a way she couldn't quite put her finger on. "Yes, Margaret told us you would be coming by." Quinn turned towards Fiona, who had risen from her chair and walked to the door to greet their guest.

"May I introduce my friend Fiona Fitzsimmons? And I'm Quinn Langston."

"It's good to meet you both. Margaret has told me so much about you. I almost feel I know you already. Margaret has such a high opinion of the two of you. I'm glad to put faces to all the wonderful stories."

Quinn momentarily wondered about the stories but put the thought out of her mind as she offered their guest some tea.

"Oh, thank you, but I just had lunch at Margaret's. I couldn't put another thing in my mouth." Hattie was now seated in one of Quinn's wingback chairs. She bent forward a little and began gently stroking Maggie's head as the little dog sniffed at her legs and feet.

Quinn wasn't sure how to proceed since she had never rented a property to anyone and didn't know what questions would be appropriate. Finally, she started with, "Margaret tells us you're retiring from a job at a detective agency in Bristol. That must have been interesting work?"

Hattie smiled her disarming smile again, "Oh, it could be occasionally, but usually it was divorce cases and the like. Most days were boring. Not nearly as exciting as the movies would have you think."

"Margaret mentioned you have a dog," said Fiona.

"Oh, yes, Wolfie, I'd be lost without him. He goes everywhere with me. He's in the car right now. I thought you might like to meet him."

"We would love to meet him," said Quinn. "I suppose you've heard that, besides Maggie here, we have a raven and two pigs, and we're thinking of adding some chickens to have our own fresh eggs." Quinn hoped the thought of a raven wouldn't frighten Hattie.

"I'm very fond of animals." Hattie gave a low whistle, which brought Pike out of the study and onto her shoulder. "Of course, Pike and I are old friends from when he lived with Daniel at their B&B." Hattie looked at ease with the bird as she reached up and stroked Pike's head. Hattie continued, "I haven't been around pigs much, though I have nothing against them. I think chickens are a wonderful idea. Fresh eggs from free-range chickens are much healthier than store-bought ones." Hattie adjusted Pike to her other shoulder before adding, "Would you like me to tell you a little about myself before you show me your guest house? I certainly would want to know whom I was renting to if I were in your place. A person can't be too careful about such things. I have learned that from my years as a detective."

Quinn felt relieved to find Hattie so understanding. "That would probably be a good way to get to know each other better if you're sure you don't mind."

"I don't mind a bit. It's such a coincidence that you talked to Margaret about renting out your guest cottage just now. I think Margaret must have told you I've been coming to Ballyfrannen for some years. My mother was from here originally, and when I was growing up, she talked about this area a lot. I don't think she ever stopped missing her home. Money was tight when I was young, though, so she didn't get to come back for a visit until I was grown. I visited for the first time about ten years ago and fell in love with the place. I could see why my mother loved it. Anyway, I always said that I would move here when I retired, and that is precisely what I plan to do. I should tell you I have a good income from my savings and respect other people's privacy. Oh, and I'm a very tidy person. I'm looking for a long let. I've thought about buying, but I don't think I want to deal with the upkeep at my age." Hattie paused, "Let's see, what else would you like to know?"

"That sounds like plenty of information for now," said Quinn. "Maybe you would like to see the cottage, and then we could meet Wolfie?" Quinn looked at Fiona for confirmation, and she gave Quinn a little nod.

As Hattie rose from the chair, Pike flew off toward the kitchen. Then, they all headed out the front door to walk the short distance to the guest house. Quinn and Fiona had to go at a trot to keep up with Hattie's long strides. She seemed remarkably fit for a woman in her fifties.

"Here we are," said Quinn as she fiddled with the keys to the cottage. Quinn and Fiona both stepped back to let Hattie enter first.

Hattie slowly walked through the cottage before turning to Quinn and Fiona. "Well, if this isn't the most perfect little cottage I've ever seen! It would be just the right size for my needs, and you've done a wonderful job restoring it. It is far lovelier than anything I had hoped to find. Now, I think you'd better meet Wolfie so you can decide whether we are what you're looking for." Hattie walked out the front door and headed toward her car.

It was then that Quinn and Fiona noticed the giant beast

sitting in the passenger seat of the small automobile. With some coaxing from Hattie, Wolfie slowly emerged from the vehicle. He was the biggest Irish Wolfhound Quinn had ever seen. He trotted alongside Hattie, keeping up easily with her long strides. If ever a human and dog were perfectly paired, it was Hattie and Wolfie.

Quinn felt Fiona poke her in the ribs. She quickly turned towards her friend and whispered, "If you say anything to make me laugh right now, I'll kill you." She wondered why Margaret hadn't seen fit to mention that Wolfie was possibly the most enormous dog on the planet.

Just then, Maggie returned from a little jaunt around the farm. Spotting the unfamiliar dog, she ran toward it. Quinn felt herself stiffen. She hurriedly called to Maggie, patting her thighs and calling her name over and over to head her off. The idea that Maggie could be devoured right before her eyes ran through her mind. Her efforts to retrieve the little dog were in vain, though, as Maggie reached Hattie and Wolfie before Quinn could get to her, and what happened next was a complete surprise.

Wolfie stood, wagging his tail, as Maggie raced towards him. When she got close, he flopped down in the grass and rolled over onto his back. His large paws dangled above him as he extended his head to sniff noses with Maggie from this very non-threatening position. When the little terrier was finished with her greeting, Wolfie got to his feet and stood looking down at her, still wagging his tail gently from side to side. He watched expectantly as Quinn approached. Then he greeted her by nuzzling his head into the crook of her arm and looking up at her with his gentle brown eyes. Quinn was utterly won over. Fiona, who got much the same treatment from Wolfie, had the same reaction.

Hattie thoughtfully walked a little ways off, pretending to

be preoccupied with the dogs, which gave Quinn and Fiona a chance to speak privately.

"I can't think of a reason in the world not to rent to her," said Fiona. "I think Hattie and Wolfie are both delightful."

"I couldn't agree more," said Quinn. "I think they are the perfect pair for our little guest house. You know, we've been talking about naming it something besides the guest house; why not call it "Hattie's Cottage?" I think that has a nice ring to it. What do you think?"

Fiona smiled and squeezed Quinn's arm, "So much better than selling it to the Tricots! Calling it Hattie's Cottage sounds just right." Fiona turned towards their cottage.

Quinn motioned for Hattie to join them, and as she did, she noticed a grey Audi slowly driving by. Through the windscreen, she could see the faces of Madeleine and Bruno Tricot. They both seemed to be glaring at her. Quinn said nothing to Fiona about seeing the couple. She was determined not to let the Tricot's spoil the day.

Quinn walked behind Fiona and Hattie into the house. After they had all seated themselves again, Quinn spoke. "Hattie, we would love to have you and Wolfie live in our guest house if you are certain that is what you want."

"Oh, I couldn't be any surer of that. I never expected to find a place as lovely as your little stone guest house to live in."

"Well, then, there's one more thing." Quinn smiled at Fiona before continuing. "Hattie, Fiona, and I have been thinking of giving the guest house a name. We hadn't been able to come up with anything until now. Would you mind if we called it Hattie's Cottage? Would that be alright with you?"

Hattie sat for a moment, blinking before answering. "My heavens, you two have touched me so, I'm just about to cry. I can't think of anything you could do to make me feel more welcome."

With that, the three gathered in the kitchen while Fiona made tea. Maggie and Wolfie watched the activity stretched out on the floor, side by side, like old friends. Pike strutted atop the refrigerator, occasionally casting a watchful eye in Wolfie's direction. Over tea, it was arranged that Hattie would send for her belongings and move in within the week. Everyone was delighted with the arrangement.

CHAPTER 21

Quinn was in a good mood as she headed into town for her morning appointments. As she approached the outskirts of Ballyfrannen, her mood changed inexplicably, and the odd feeling that she had been having quite a lot lately returned. Something felt almost sinister, though she couldn't think what. She tried to shake the feeling off to no avail. As she drove nearer the clinic, she spotted two Garda vehicles parked out front, and the bad feeling turned into outright fear. What could have happened to require such a turn-out? Then, she noticed the yellow police tape that stretched around the entire entryway of the clinic.

Quinn quickly parked and hopped out of her car. She approached the clinic and began to lift an edge of the police tape when she heard Dermot Brennan shout at her. "Stop right there, Missus. No one's allowed beyond this point."

"Excuse me, Officer Brennan, but I work here. Has there been a robbery?"

"Nothing as mundane as a robbery." Dermot lifted his head importantly and hitched up his trousers before continuing. "A robbery would be child's play compared to what's happened here."

Quinn was running out of patience, "Dermot, could you just tell me what is going on, please?"

Dermot's shoulders slumped. "Well, Missus, there's been a murder committed right here in this clinic, that's what. You can't come in here either. This is a crime scene, and only the police are allowed in until everything is secured."

"A murder! Dear God, who was killed?"

"Well, I guess it will do no harm to tell you. It was Nola Baird. She was killed right there in that front office last evening. She was working late. Someone shot her in the back through that open window. Cathal Fagan found her first thing this morning. She was slumped over the desk with just a little reading light on. Her husband hadn't even realized she didn't come home last night. He had turned in early after getting the kids to bed. He didn't report her missing until this morning, but Cathal had already found her by then. I wasn't the one who had to tell him his wife was dead, thank God." Dermot crossed himself and paced nervously as he spoke.

Quinn was too horrified to speak. The window Dermot had pointed to was the one in her office. She could see Fiona's potted Geraniums looking bright and cheery through the open window. Nola had called her yesterday to ask if she could use Quinn's office for the day while hers was being painted, and now Nola was dead—Nola, who had a husband and three small children waiting for her at home. She had been killed right here at the clinic, in Quinn's office. Quinn couldn't take it all in.

Everything began to look fuzzy, and there was a funny whirring noise in her ears. She felt herself fall forward as two strong arms grabbed her from behind. The last thing she remembered was hearing Colin's voice calling her name.

When Quinn woke, she was lying on the small sofa in the clinic's waiting room. Colin and Cathal stood over her, talking quietly. When Colin saw her eyes open, he bent down to stroke her head.

"You gave us a scare, fainting like that. It's a good thing I was there to catch you." Their eyes held for a long moment, and then Quinn made to get up.

"I think you should lie here a few more minutes, Quinn; you're still as white as a sheet," Cathal's calm voice seemed to restore some order to Quinn's mind.

She looked at Colin, who was still stroking her head, "Is it true? Is Nola dead?"

"I'm afraid so, Quinn. None of us can believe it. Who would want to harm poor Nola? The woman didn't have had an enemy in the world."

Quinn finally sat up. She was still feeling shaky and weak, but she couldn't just lie there with everyone standing over her. Colin sat down beside her and reached for her hand. "Are you sure you're okay?"

"I'll be fine, Colin. It was just such a shock. I still can't believe Nola was murdered." Quinn took a ragged breath before continuing. "Colin, I think that bullet was meant for me."

The look on Colin's face said that he was thinking the same thing. "Quinn, I think we had better talk to Dermot's superior about everything that has happened to you."

Quinn nodded in agreement. "Do you think the Tricots are capable of such a thing?"

Colin shook his head. "I don't know what to think anymore, Quinn. I just know I want you to be safe." The tenderness on his face was almost more than Quinn could bear.

After Quinn gave the officer in charge all the information regarding the two incidents with the silver car, Colin walked her to her car. As she drove home, she thought about the officer's reaction when she told him she had already given Dermot Brennan the information she was giving him and that he had failed to take her seriously. She suspected Dermot would hear about that. What did it all mean, though? If the bullet that killed Nola had been meant for her, who had fired it? Why would someone want to kill her?

CHAPTER 22

*I*t was three days before the clinic was allowed to re-open. Quinn was surprised that Megan Murphy was her first patient of the day. She was glad the girl had resumed counseling.

Quinn sat in her office, trying not to think about what had happened to Nola in this very room such a short time ago. Megan sat across from her.

"I'm glad to see you again, Megan. I was afraid you had stopped treatment for good. What brought you back just now?" Quinn tried to sound normal.

Megan fidgeted in her chair for a moment before saying, "Well, Dr. Langston, to be honest, I'm having a hard time dealing with the fact that Thomas has decided not to marry me. I was so certain that he loved me and that we would be together forever." Megan raised her eyes to look in Quinn's direction.

"I know it is hard when someone leaves, Megan, especially in your circumstance. You have had so many other losses. Try to look at it from a positive perspective, though. If you and Thomas weren't meant to be together, isn't it better to find that out before you married?"

"I don't know, Dr. Langston. All I know is I love him, and I'm not okay with this."

Quinn changed the subject, "Megan, what else has been happening in your life?"

"Nothing really, Dr. Langston. Same old job, same bad relationship with my mother." Megan paused before adding, "I truly miss my grandmother; she was the only person I could talk to." Megan looked down at her lap.

Quinn's heart went out to her. She was glad that Megan had resumed counseling. She would do all she could to help her.

Quinn arrived home to find Margaret, Fiona, and Hattie gathered around the kitchen table. She could hear their chatter as she walked through the front door, which cheered her a little. She continued into the kitchen and purposely smiled cheerfully as she greeted her friends.

Margaret jumped up from the table and began fussing over Quinn. "Have you had your tea? I've brought over some leftover chicken casserole if you're hungry."

Fiona added, "It's delicious, Quinn. You should have some."

Quinn hadn't missed the looks being passed around the table; that said, they were all concerned about her well-being. Quinn sat down and smiled with genuine gratitude. "I'm really fine, but I appreciate all of you more than you know."

Fiona scooped spoonfuls of chicken casserole onto a plate and sat it down in front of Quinn. "You may be fine, but you still need to eat."

Margaret brought a cup of tea and set it down next to the plate of chicken. Then she gave Quinn a little pat on the shoulder before sitting back down.

Hattie was the next to speak, "Quinn, have you heard anything more about the murder? Are they any closer to discovering who did it? I don't suppose they have much to go on since whoever it was wasn't even in the room. Did they find any footprints under the window, fingerprints, on the windowsill, anything?" Then Hattie caught herself, "Quinn, I'm so sorry. My questions are probably upsetting you. It's just the detective in me, I guess."

Quinn smiled as she took a small bite of casserole. "It's okay, Hattie. I keep trying to get information myself, but so far, I haven't been able to find out anything. I don't know if that means they don't know anything or that they don't want to discuss an ongoing investigation."

Fiona passed Quinn the milk and sugar for her tea and added, "Well, I hope they aren't expecting Dermot Brennan to solve anything. I'm still mad that he didn't take Quinn seriously when she told him what was happening to her. I was in his mother's shop yesterday and told her what an idiot I thought her son was."

Quinn couldn't help laughing, "Fiona, you didn't?"

"Oh, yes, I did. I would tell him to his face. And I just might, the next time I see him."

Quinn changed the subject. "Margaret, would you be willing to help us find some laying hens? We thought we would put them in the shed next to Tam and Hilda's."

"How many do you think you would want? I think five or six would be plenty myself." Margaret pursed her lips and looked up at the ceiling, mentally calculating. "Were ye thinking more?"

"We trust your opinion on the matter, Margaret," said Quinn. "I have no idea how many eggs a chicken lays or how often."

Margaret still seemed to be thinking. "Well, that all

depends on the hen, of course. Ye should get all you need from six hens, though. And, of course, ye need a rooster."

'Why do we need a rooster?' Fiona looked perplexed.

"Where do ye think the eggs come from, ye eejit? Ye do realize the eggs are baby chickens, for heaven's sake!"

Hattie snorted and almost spit out her tea. Even Quinn had to laugh. "Fiona, I know we're city girls, but come on!"

Okay, okay, I wasn't thinking, alright?

Unintentionally, but to everyone's relief, Fiona had lightened the mood.

Margaret shook her head one last time, "I'll put Daniel on it tomorrow if ye want them right away?"

Fiona shrugged her shoulders, still feeling sheepish, "Sure, why not? As long as Daniel is willing to give us a little instruction on caring for and feeding chickens. We're experts now regarding ravens or pigs, but we still know nothing about chickens...which I guess is obvious!"

"There's no big fuss to raising a few chickens; Daniel will have ye sorted in no time." Margaret smiled, "You two are turning into regular farmers. Hattie, are you sure you're ready for life on a farm with us three eejits as friends?"

It was Hattie's turn to smile. "You know, Margaret, there isn't a day that goes by that I don't feel thankful to have found the three of you, and as for this farm, I think it's the most wonderful place on earth."

All four women sat quietly for a moment, each feeling lucky to have found such great friends.

Two days later, a moving van pulled up to the little guest house, now renamed Hattie's Cottage. Quinn, Fiona, and Margaret all helped Hattie unpack and arrange furniture.

As Quinn unpacked a small box, she noticed a framed photo of a magazine cover. Quinn recognized the name as one of Europe's most popular and prestigious fashion magazines. The glamorous woman in the picture was dressed in the fashion of the late eighties. She was stunningly beautiful. Quinn studied the photo. Something about the model's smile seemed familiar, and then it hit her. Quinn was staring at a picture of the young Hattie Biggs! The features, which now seemed overly large, had, in her youth, been striking. Her hair, in the photo, was long and thick, and her face was expertly made up. Dark eyeliner framed her eyes and made them luminous. The caption of the photo said the model's name was Antonia.

Quinn walked over to Hattie, who was helping Fiona position a chair by the fireplace. Speechless, she handed the photo to Hattie and looked up at her wide-eyed. Hattie took the picture and casually glanced at it before handing it back to Quinn. "I think I'll just leave that in the box it was packed in."

As Hattie turned back to the chair, Quinn finally found her voice. "Hattie, you were a famous model? Your name used to be Antonia?"

Fiona looked up as she let go of the chair. "Who was a model, named what?"

Quinn handed Fiona the framed photo, and her reaction was much the same as Quinn's. She stood staring at the magazine cover with her mouth open.

Margaret chimed in, "What's this about a model?" She took the photo from Fiona, and she, too, stood in open-mouthed amazement.

Hattie looked at the three of them and began to laugh. "You know, I could almost be offended by your reactions. Even I was young once. Is it so hard to believe that I used to be young and beautiful? Do I look that bad?"

Quinn was the first to speak. "Hattie, you look just fine, but you could have mentioned that you were a famous model when you were young."

Fiona looked at the picture again before adding, "If I had

looked like that in my youth, I would make sure the whole world knew about it."

Margaret kept looking back and forth between the picture and Hattie. "Hattie Biggs, in all the years we have known each other, you've never mentioned a thing about this."

Hattie sat down in the chair she and Fiona had been moving and sighed deeply, "Some things are better left in the past, I guess. When I look at that picture, I only see a lot of terrible memories. What a fool I was back then. I ended up broken-hearted and alone."

Quinn pulled a kitchen chair over and sat down near Hattie. "Do you feel like telling us what happened?"

Hattie sighed again, "I might as well; the three of you will pester me until I do." She smiled, but her sadness was palpable.

Fiona and Margaret each found a chair and sat down as Hattie continued speaking.

"I started modeling when I was eighteen. I guess you could say I was pretty successful at it. At one time, I was one of the top five models in the country." Hattie laughed a little self-consciously before continuing. "It's been a while since I've spoken with anyone about this. It all seems such a long time ago now." Hattie looked up for a moment before continuing. "When I was twenty-two, I was given a modeling assignment in France. On my first day of shooting, I met a young man; he was one of the photographers I was working with. He was tall, good-looking, and smart. I was smitten from the moment we were introduced. After finishing the shoot, we all went to dinner to celebrate. After that, we went to a nightclub. He and I danced and talked all evening, and somehow, I just knew that this was the only man I would ever love. I was sure he felt the same way about me. From then on, we were inseparable. We moved into a little flat in

Paris. A few months later, he asked me to marry him. I was beside myself with joy. We planned a small wedding with just my family and our closest friends as guests. His parents had died a few years before we'd met, and he had no other family. We had a little celebration the night before we were to be married. Our friends took turns making toasts to our future happiness. Then, we kissed goodnight, and he went off, saying it was bad luck to spend the night before our wedding with his bride-to-be. That was the last time I ever saw him. I waited for hours in the small chapel we had chosen in the French countryside, thinking he would still come long after the guests had gone. I couldn't believe he had deserted me like that. How could I have been so stupid to believe he had loved me the way I loved him? I was inconsolable. He had just vanished. No one knew where he was or what had happened to him. I gave up modeling and trying to be glamorous. What was the point? To this very day, I still don't know what happened. I think that's why I became a private detective. Deep down, I always hoped I'd find some answers."

Margaret was the first to speak. "Hattie, I'm so sorry. I had no idea. I wish you'd said."

"There was no point in talking about it. I've had a good life. Still, have a good life. And I'm grateful to be here in Ballyfrannen with all of you. That part of me is gone forever. I'm not Antonia; that was just the name my modeling agency chose for me. I'm just plain old Hattie Biggs." Hattie rose from her chair. "Now, are you three going to help me finish moving in or not?"

CHAPTER 23

The next morning, Quinn sat in her office dreading her session with Jozef Abram. She hoped it would not go like the last one. She knew he was already sitting in the waiting room. Finally, she called him in.

"Hello, Jozef. Are you feeling any better today?"

"I am feeling better than the last time I was here, I guess. My wife did not go with her mother to Poland. She says she will give me another chance if I continue to come to the clinic and see you. My wife, she, has great faith in psychologists." Jozef said the last in a way that implied he didn't share her sentiments.

"I'm glad your family is still together, Jozef. Shall we work on some imagery that might help manage your anger?"

Jozef seemed cooperative enough, and the session passed without incident.

After Jozef left, Quinn sat staring out her window. She had to admit she hadn't felt comfortable in her office since Nola's death. Cathal had offered her Nola's old office, but that didn't feel right either. Just then, she heard a light tap at her door.

"Quinn, am I disturbing you?"

Quinn pulled herself out of her reverie and looked up to see Hattie's tall frame in the doorway. "No, of course not, Hattie. Come in and have a seat. I don't have any more patients today. Why don't we both have a cup of tea? I think I've got some biscuits somewhere if you'd like one."

"That would be great if you're sure I'm not disturbing you. I just thought this would be a way to speak to you privately about Nola Baird's murder. I don't want to upset Fiona and Margaret more than they already are. But I've been doing a lot of thinking, Quinn, and I'm worried that whoever it was will try again, and I don't mean to let that happen. I've solved more than a few murders in my time."

Quinn appreciated Hattie's offer of help. She certainly didn't have much confidence in Dermot Brennan's abilities. She knew there were others on the case besides Dermot, but what would it hurt to let Hattie do some investigating, too? "Hattie, I would be grateful to have your help. Are you sure you want to get involved, though?"

"Quinn, since moving to Ballyfrannen, I consider you and Fiona to be two of my dearest friends, and besides, what else do I have to do? I'm all moved in, and I'm not one to just sit. I would be discreet, of course. People assume a woman my age asking questions is just an old busybody. It works to my advantage." Hattie laughed, and Quinn again noticed the transformation in her face.

Quinn poured Hattie some tea and placed some biscuits on a plate. "Alright, Hattie, if you're certain?"

"Oh, I'm certain, Quinn. I'll get started first thing tomorrow morning."

Hattie decided to start her investigation with the Tricots. It wasn't hard to find out where they were staying. Conversation at Coughlin's Grocery led to talk of the famous couple and the fact that they had rented a luxury, self-catering property at the edge of town. Hattie wasted no time in driving out to visit them. She had already decided that she would say she planned to rent the same property herself in a few months, and she was stopping by to see if they were happy with the accommodation.

Hattie pulled into the driveway and sat for a moment, collecting her thoughts. Lying was a bit of an art, and she considered herself good at it. She hated to admit it, but she had always enjoyed pretending to be someone she wasn't. Today, she would be a wealthy widow with three grown children, planning a holiday for all of them here in Ballyfrannen. Yes, that would do nicely.

Hattie pulled at the knocker on the large wooden door. The house was really lovely. It was a period property with tall windows overlooking a large, well-kept garden. This must rent for a pretty penny, she thought, just as the front door opened. A tall, striking woman of about forty had opened the door.

"Yes, may I help you, Madame?"

There was no missing the fact that this woman was once a model, thought Hattie. She could spot one a mile away! Something about the way they carried themselves, she guessed.

"Yes, I believe you can. My name is Elizabeth Hollis." Hattie spoke in a cultured, upper-class voice and adopted a bit of an arrogant manner, like a woman used to getting her way. "You see, my grown children and I will be renting this property in a few months, and I wondered if you have been satisfied with the accommodation. My main residence is in London, of course, and I also own a villa in the south of France, but we wanted to do something different this year. I find Ballyfrannen such a charming little town. I thought the grandchildren might enjoy a long stay."

Madeleine studied her for a moment. "You are very tall, Madame. Have you ever done any modeling?"

Hattie was caught off guard by the question. "Why yes, as a matter of fact, I have. It was a very long time ago, though. I'm sure you would never have heard of me."

"No, I do not remember a model by the name of... Elizabeth Hollis, is it?" Madeleine continued staring intently at Hattie.

"Yes, that's right," Hattie was getting more uncomfortable by the minute.

"Wait, I have it now! You are Antonia! You modeled in the early 90s. I am right, no?" Madeleine looked pleased with herself. "I have collected dee fashion magazines since I was a little girl. I know every model who was ever on the cover of a major magazine. Come in, please. I am happy to show you the house. My name is Madeleine Tricot, by the way. It was Madeleine Oberon when I was modeling; you have heard of me, yes?"

"Of course," lied Hattie. She followed Madeleine through the large, ornate foyer into a lovely, paneled room at the front of the house that served as the lounge. The furniture looked comfortable and expensive. Madeleine offered her a seat. Hattie tried to quickly analyze this turn of events before proceeding. Just stick to the story you started with, she told herself. Antonia could just as easily have turned into Elizabeth Hollis as Hattie Biggs. This woman will never know the difference.

"Now, what can I get for you, Madame? Would you like tea or a cocktail?"

"Tea would be fine if you're sure it's no bother. I hope I'm not inconveniencing you by stopping by like this." Hattie took pains to speak with an upper-class English accent.

"Not at all... Elizabeth. May I call you Elizabeth?"

Madeleine seemed pleased with this unexpected visit from someone with whom she had so much in common.

"Of course, of course," Hattie smiled warmly at Madeleine. "We are sisters, after all. Not many women get to experience what we have." That was true enough, thought Hattie.

"Well, Elizabeth, I am only sorry you will not get to meet my husband today. You have heard of him, no doubt. He is dee famous documentary filmmaker Bruno Tricot. He is meeting with dee Building Permission Society this morning. We bought a wonderful large piece of land on dee sea near here some time ago, but we have been unable to build on it. They have such stupid rules here in Ireland regarding such things. I tell you, Madame, do not buy any land in this country if you do not have building permission first! What we have been through has been a nightmare."

Hattie took advantage of the opening by saying, "Please tell me about your experience."

Madeleine looked dismayed, "Truly, Madame, it is too horrible to dwell on. All would have gone well if those two dreadful women who live on the land next to ours had sold us their horrible little guest cottage. Owning that would have solved everything, but they are the most selfish women I have ever encountered. They have made everything so difficult for us." Madeleine sat back in her chair as though worn out from speaking. "We have triumphed in the end, though. The Building Permission Society called a few days ago to say they had worked it all out. My husband is there now, obtaining dee paperwork. Now, let me get our tea, and we will become better acquainted." With that, Madeleine headed towards the back of the house, leaving Hattie alone to digest the information.

Since the Building Permission Society had called before Nola was murdered, the Tricots would have had no motive to harm Quinn. Hattie would visit The Building Society and get an exact date when they had called to make sure.

When Madeleine returned, they sat discussing their modeling days until Hattie could comfortably excuse herself by saying she had forgotten about another appointment.

Madeleine was a little annoyed that Elizabeth Hollis had left so abruptly. She would have liked a longer chat with the former Antonia. After all, how often did she get to talk about her days as a model anymore? Madeleine wanted to consider herself to have been a supermodel, but in fact, she hadn't been nearly as famous as Antonia. Why had the woman abandoned her career so suddenly? She had stopped modeling in her early twenties when she was still at the height of her career. Madeleine couldn't conceive of such a thing. She had only stopped when the work had completely dried up.

Madeline poured herself a strong drink and sat down to wait for her husband. Finally, she thought, I will have the beautiful house by the sea I have always dreamed of. She sat, envisioning the fantastic house she would build. She would spare no cost in building this dream home. After all, if she were honest, she had only married Bruno because he was rich and famous. He had always given her everything she wanted, and now her dream of a home by the sea would also come true.

Just then, Madeleine heard her husband's key in the door. She arranged herself artfully on the chair to look her best when he came in. For once, she was glad to see him. She could hear his somewhat shuffling footsteps as he approached the lounge. "Hello, darling. Would you care to join me for a drink to celebrate our success?"

Madeleine's voice was grating to Bruno's ears. Why was she only in a good mood when she thought she was getting something? He felt a slight sensation of pleasure as he thought of the news he was about to deliver.

"Madeleine, I have something to tell you that you're not going to like ..."

Bruno explained to his wife that their finances were depleted from years of overspending and that the home they would be building would have to be much smaller and simpler than the one she had envisioned. They'd also have to sell their other assets to pay back taxes. Now, they would need to make do with a small retirement fund he had managed to keep out of her hands.

Bruno had hoped to make one last documentary before retiring. It would have been more commercial than most of his other films and would have paid handsomely, but that had fallen through when the backers had withdrawn from the project. He had no other offers of work, and since his last two projects had lost money, he had no illusions that, at his age, there would be other offers. Besides, he was tired of roaming the globe, working in uncomfortable locations to make movies that nobody seemed to care about. He was ready to build a small house here in Ireland and try to live the remaining years of his life in peace.

Madeleine sat in stunned silence. Finally, she spoke, "And to think I thought this would be such a good day. This afternoon was so enjoyable. I was paid a visit by Antonia, a former supermodel like me. We had such fun reliving our days in the spotlight, and now you come home and spoil everything. Well, I have had enough. I am leaving you, Bruno! I will go back to France this very day. There is no use trying to stop me." With that, Madeleine marched up the stairs to pack her bags.

Now it was Bruno's turn to be shocked. His wife's words had completely unnerved him. Not that he cared she was leaving. He was relieved to hear that, actually. What feelings he'd had for her had long since died. But she said she had seen Antonia. Had Antonia really been in this very room a short time ago? His thoughts went back to the life he had led before he had taken the name Tricot and become a filmmaker.

He had been an underpaid photographer with a weakness for gambling when, as a young man, he had met Antonia. Antonia had come to Paris on a modeling assignment, and he was one of the photographers hired for the shoot. Bruno hadn't been able to take his eyes off her. She had been such a lovely and trusting young girl—too trusting. He knew how much money successful models like Antonia earned.

He wasted no time in pursuing her. They spent their days walking around Paris, hand in hand. And their nights in small cafes drinking wine and making plans for their future. He filled her mind with stories of the kind of life they could have together. A life full of adventure and traveling the world together.

But he was also thinking that if they were married, he would have enough money to pay off his debts and, finally, be able to work on the documentary-type films he so desperately wanted to make.

At the last moment, though, his conscience had got the better of him. He didn't go through with the wedding. Instead, he had caught a freighter and drifted around the world for several years. Finally, he was able to scrape together enough money to make his first film.

He changed his name to Tricot and was careful not to be photographed. People chalked it off to eccentricity, but Bruno secretly feared being found out by the people he owed money to in Paris. They were not the kind of people to be forgiving.

He had almost forgotten about the foolish young man he had been so many years ago, but hearing of Antonia brought it all back. She was the reason he had been drawn to this area in the first place. Antonia had often said that someday she would live in Ballyfrannen. To be told she was here was almost more than he could bear. Too late, he had realized how much he loved her. He had wanted to go back and tell her the truth, but he never had the courage, and then she faded from sight. No one knew why she had stopped modeling. As the years passed, he was too ashamed to try to find her. Instead, he tried to forget about her and continue his life. He had married three times. All had been models, like Antonia, but none had been Antonia, so the marriages had failed.

CHAPTER 24

*Q*uinn and Fiona went on as usual. Neither wanted to mention the murder of Nola Baird or the fact that whoever had murdered her might strike again. Instead, they sought distraction. They decided to proceed with the hens. They poured over countless books that described the different breeds. Which laid the most eggs, which had the best temperament, which tended to be the healthiest? Finally, they decided on a breed called Orpingtons. They were not only prolific layers but also resilient to cold weather.

Fiona and Daniel spent the better part of a day turning the last remaining out house into a chicken coop. Daniel built three nest boxes so each hen would have her laying area. Then, they made a large enclosure, knowing that the breed they had chosen required a lot of space to roam. They then purchased three hens and one rooster. Quinn and Fiona found the constant clucking a pleasant enough sound. Theirs was a real working farm now, and they felt proud. Even the orchard was producing. They had apples, plums, cherries, and pears in abundance. Some would be used for canning and fresh fruit, and the rest would be sold to Coughlin's Grocery. Both women took pleasure in what they had accomplished in the year since they had bought Raven Hill Farm.

Hattie sat by the window in the sitting room of her small cottage, lost in thought. She had checked with the Building Permission Society. They had given her the date the Tricots were told they could build on their property. It was the day before Nola Baird's murder. That ruled them out as suspects.

Hattie felt she now must investigate the people who came to Quinn seeking therapy. Quinn was not allowed to discuss her patients, but Hattie could still do some spying. She had a way of finding things out. Hattie knew that time was of the essence. A feeling in her gut told her that whoever it was would try again and soon.

THE DAY WAS overcast and chilly. The wind blew in unpleasant gusts, causing Hattie to button her coat and pull the old hat she was wearing a little further down on her head. She had been sitting on the bench across from the Mental Health Clinic on and off for three days. Today, she had forgotten to bring a cushion, and she was finding the wooden bench more uncomfortable by the minute. She knew, though, that Quinn was having a therapy session with Agnes Meek and she wanted to follow the woman when she came out.

It hadn't been hard to gather information on Quinn's patients. Hattie had followed each one as they left the clinic, and from there, it had been easy to discover their identity and do some checking on them.

Hattie had learned a lot about Jozef Abram. She knew he was a Polish immigrant who had been in this country for a little over a year. Jozef had a wife and two children, whom he berated and physically abused. Also, he served several months in prison in Poland, after being convicted of assault. From all she could gather, he had a savage temper and raged when angry. Other patients' histories also disturbed Hattie.

The woman Quinn was now seeing had an interesting past. Agnes Meek was seven when her three-year-old sister drowned under questionable circumstances. Agnes had always been a little off, according to people Hattie had spoken to about her. She had become estranged from her parents by her late teens and had no friends to speak of.

Had her parents thought Agnes was responsible for her sister's death? Hattie had heard about Agnes winning the lottery some years back and how that had, strangely led to a massive weight gain. She seemed, by all accounts, to be quite mentally unstable.

Megan Murphy was a young woman who seemed straightforward enough. She was a troubled girl but harmless. Her boyfriend, though, was another matter. Thomas Lafferty was the type of person who might harm someone if he felt he had a reason. His family life had been horrible. His brother was in prison for selling drugs, his mother was an alcoholic whose treatment of her children had, no doubt, been abusive and neglectful, and his father had disappeared altogether. The brewery owner where Thomas had worked until recently said he was obsessed and overly possessive of his girlfriend. He had bragged to a co-worker that he was seeing Megan's therapist to find out what they discussed. He had also said he was sure the therapist was out to break them up and that if she did, she would live to regret it.

Hattie felt that Jozef, Agnes, and Thomas could all be capable of murder. She would make it her business to monitor all of them. She could only hope the Garda were doing the same.

Quinn sat in her office, absently rubbing her left temple.

She was trying to focus on what Agnes was saying. Since the murder of Nola Baird, Quinn found it hard to concentrate on anything.

However, it hadn't escaped her notice that Hattie had been camped out across the street. She found her presence comforting. She wondered how much information Hattie had managed to gather regarding her patients. Hattie probably knew as much about them as she did, Quinn guessed. Could one of them really have murdered Nola?

Quinn realized that Agnes was speaking. "Dr. Langston, I don't think you're listening to what I'm saying!" Agnes had an angry look on her face.

"I'm sorry, Agnes. I guess I have a lot on my mind. I think I missed what you said just now."

Agnes' face relaxed, "Oh, never mind, it wasn't of consequence, anyway."

Quinn looked closely at Agnes for a moment, "You know, Agnes, I think you've made some real progress lately. Just look at you. I'm sure you've lost a great deal of weight."

Agnes looked pleased, "I was wondering when you would notice! I've lost over forty pounds in the last few months. I guess our sessions have done me a lot of good. Those bad dreams have let up, too. The last time I dreamed of seeing my sister in the stream, she looked up at me and said, ' This isn't your fault.'

"I woke up feeling close to Emily and remembering the way it was before she died." Agnes sighed deeply before adding, "You know I never cried for Emily."

"Why was that, Agnes?" Quinn felt a deep pain of empathy building in her stomach.

"My mother said it was my fault that Emily died. She said she had better never catch me crying because girls who killed their little sisters didn't have a right to cry. So, I never did, and I never felt bad after that either. It was as if it had never happened; I felt nothing."

"Agnes, are you telling me you never grieved for your sister? Surely, you know how wrong it was of your mother to blame you for her death. You were just a little girl yourself; how could you be responsible for a three-year-old?"

"But my mother told me to watch her, and I didn't."

Quinn had never seen such sadness on Agnes's face. "Agnes, don't you see whose fault it was that your sister died? Don't you see who really should have been watching her? What right did your mother have to blame a seven-year-old? What right did she have to steal your grief?"

Agnes sat blinking for a few moments. "You really believe it wasn't my fault, Dr. Langston?"

"I don't just believe it, Agnes. I know it." Quinn smiled and pulled two tissues from their box, one for Agnes and one for herself. She couldn't believe the cruelty some parents inflicted on their children.

Tears were sliding down Agnes's plump, heavily made-up cheeks. Then she began to sob. Her still large shoulders shook from the intensity of her emotions.

"I missed my sister so much after she died. I did love her, I still do, and I miss her every day." Agnes's shoulders again began to heave with emotion. "I've felt like such a bad person all my life. I didn't blame my mother for not loving me, but... you can't imagine how alone I felt, how alone I still feel after all these years." Agnes's face finally held all the grief she had been burying.

"You don't have to be alone anymore, Agnes. Now that you know the truth, you can begin to heal. You have already begun to do that; that takes a lot of courage. I'm proud of you for how far you've come."

Agnes smiled, probably the first genuine smile Quinn had ever seen from Agnes. Quinn felt that she was meeting Agnes for the first time, and in a way, she was. This was the real Agnes—the Agnes who had been buried underneath all the hurt and guilt. Gone were the odd mannerisms, the constant being in motion, and the excessive blinking and blank stare. A real person sat looking at Quinn.

Quinn never ceased to be amazed at the cruelty some children endured. Seemly, ordinary people could do so much damage to those around them. Agnes had been unlucky enough to have just such a person for a mother. Quinn knew that this woman must also have suffered emotional hurt of some kind to have behaved the way she had, but it was hard for Quinn not to feel dislike for such an abusive mother. She had given her child a lifelong sentence of suffering and guilt, and the consequences for Agnes had been severe. She had never really experienced the everyday pleasures others took for granted. Quinn had great hope that now she would have that chance.

CHAPTER 25

*Q*uinn's next patient was Megan Murphy. Megan had told her on her last visit that she was, again, having panic attacks. She said she also hadn't been sleeping well and was barely able to function at all. Today, she seemed more listless than ever. She sat nervously, clenching and unclenching her fists. Her nails were bitten down to the quick. Quinn was worried about the girl.

Megan's shoulders slumped, and she avoided eye contact with Quinn as her session began. Quinn spoke reassuringly.

"Megan, it's so good to see you again. The last time you were here, you said you had started taking the anti-anxiety medication the doctor prescribed. Is it helping at all?"

Megan looked at Quinn with a dead expression on her face. "No, Dr. Langston, nothing helps. I don't think I can go on like this much longer. I miss Thomas so much. I've tried to contact him, but he won't have anything to do with me. My mother is always at me to move back in with her, but I'd never do that. I don't know how long I'll be able to keep my job, though. I've missed so much work, and even when I'm there, I always make mistakes; I worry that they'll fire me soon."

Megan began to sob softly. Quinn moved her chair closer to the girl. "You know I'll help in any way I can, Megan. Have you tried the breathing exercises we talked about?"

Megan listened, but Quinn felt her words were having no effect.

Finally, the session was over, and Megan got up to leave. As she did, she stopped to stare at Quinn's desk. "Was that woman murdered there, at that desk?" She asked.

"Nola Baird was murdered in this office, but my desk was moved into storage. This is the desk Nola used in her office." Quinn hoped she wasn't upsetting the fragile girl.

Quinn tried to shake off thoughts of Nola's murder as she waited for her next patient. It was someone new. Quinn scanned down the brief form that each new patient filled out. She wanted to clear her thoughts as she prepared for the session. She looked at her watch. At least this was the last patient of the day. She hated the fact that she felt so little enthusiasm for her work.

Quinn drove home with a heavy heart. Maybe it had been a mistake to start a practice here in Ballyfrannen. Her life at the farm was fulfilling, after all. Why couldn't that be enough? She had missed being a psychologist after her retirement back in the States, though. And she truly did enjoy helping people. Once Nola's murderer was caught, she hoped she would feel better about everything.

QUINN ENTERED the cottage and threw her keys on the shelf by the door. Fiona must be out back tending to the animals, she thought, as she saw no sign of her in the house. She went to the back door and called her but got no answer. She might be too far away to hear, she thought.

Maggie came running in through the open door, panting, more excited than usual. Quinn stooped to pet the small dog before washing her hands and making herself a sandwich. Pike flew in through a window and perched on the refrigerator. He, too, seemed agitated, strutting back and forth as he watched her slice the ham and pour herself a glass of milk. Quinn thought, again, how thankful she was for the animals in her life. She would truly be lost without Maggie and Pike, and for that matter, Tam and Hilda. She chuckled, thinking about how tempted she and Fiona had been to give the chickens names. Certainly, Margaret would have thought them daft, but even the chickens held a place in her affection.

As Quinn sat at the kitchen table and began eating, her thoughts turned to Megan Murphy. She wished she knew how to help the girl. She had seemed so interested in Nola's murder, but Quinn supposed that was natural.

Where was Fiona anyway? Quinn finished her sandwich and decided to go looking for her. After checking all the sheds and walking to the back of the property, she began to worry. It wasn't like Fiona to leave without letting her know where she would be. Besides, her car was still in the lane.

Quinn walked back into the house, feeling more and more anxious. She entered Fiona's study and stood, scanning the room before realizing some furniture looked as though it had been shoved back. Fiona's desk was pushed a few feet from where it usually stood, and her overstuffed chair sat at an awkward angle. Quinn walked over and stood by the desk. She saw that someone had written, "Now you will know how it feels to lose someone you love," in a childish scrawl in bright red lipstick on Fiona's desk calendar. Quinn felt a chill go up her spine. What in heaven was going on? Quinn's phone rang, and she ran to pick it up.

"Fiona, is that you?"

"No, it's Hattie. Is everything okay, Quinn? You sound upset."

"I can't find Fiona anywhere, and that's not all. It looks like there was a scuffle in Fiona's study, and someone wrote, 'Now you will know how it feels to lose someone you love' on her desk calendar. Hattie, I'm afraid something terrible has happened to Fiona!"

"I'm calling the Garda right now. Stay where you are, Quinn, and don't let anyone into the house."

Hattie was trying to keep her voice calm. "Quinn, did you hear what I said?" There was no answer. Hattie realized the phone had gone dead.

Hattie put her foot down hard on the accelerator and barreled toward Raven Hill Farm. She had called the Garda and explained everything to that dolt, Dermot Brendan. She could only hope he had taken her seriously and was on his way to the farm.

Something hard poked Quinn's back, startling her. "Turn around, Dr. Langston." Quinn turned slowly. Megan Murphy was standing in front of her, holding a gun. Was that Megan Murphy, or was she hallucinating? This person didn't seem timid or fragile at all. "Put down your phone, Dr. Langston."

Quinn did as she was told. Her mind raced as she tried to figure out what was happening. "Megan, what on earth are you doing? Why do you have a gun?"

"I thought you had all the answers, Dr. Langston. Have you lost your touch, or were you always just an incompetent old windbag? Do you really have no idea what you've done to me?"

"No, Megan, I have no idea what I've done except try to help you." Quinn was still so thrown off she couldn't think straight.

"Help me! That's a laugh! You thought you were so smart, figuring out I had panic attacks because my gram died."

Megan smiled, but her eyes had a cold, dead look to them. "Well, that was partly true, I guess. I was so afraid I would get caught for pushing the old crow down the stairs; it made me nervous. She knew I was the one who set the fire that killed my father. She was going to tell the Garda. Can you imagine my own gram saying that? She deserved to die."

Quinn still couldn't seem to wrap her mind around what was happening. "Megan, you're telling me you killed your father and your grandmother; how can that be true?"

"You tell me, Doc. You're the one who's supposed to know all about this stuff."

"I finally tracked my father down about a year ago. He was roaring drunk when he answered the door. When he realized who I was, he just laughed in my face and said he never cared a thing about any of us. He was glad to be rid of my brother and me. He said we were a couple of little brats, and he couldn't stand the sight of us, so one day, he just walked out the door and never came back."

"After he slammed the door in my face, I sat in my car thinking about what a fool I'd been to think he would be glad to see me. That's when I decided to get even. I waited for him to finish drinking himself senseless, and then I sneaked back into his rathole of a house. He was passed out on the bed by then, so I set it on fire with him in it." Megan had a self-satisfied sneer on her face.

Quinn took a good look at the girl standing in front of her. She bore so little resemblance to the Megan Murphy she thought she knew. This person was a true sociopath. No amount of pleading or reasoning would have any effect. Quinn knew she needed to stay calm. She had to find out where Fiona was. She took a deep breath and tried to collect her thoughts. Hopefully, Hattie and the Garda would be there soon. She said a silent prayer for Fiona.

She would try to keep Megan talking until the Garda arrived. "Megan, you said I took something away from you?"

"Yeah, that's exactly right, Doc. You took Thomas away from me. He was the only person who really loved me, and then you turned him against me. I gave you several warnings when you started to put doubts in his mind about me. Remember the car that almost hit you when you were crossing the street? Boy, did you look scared!" Megan chuckled.

"And then there was the little incident on the country road. But you didn't get the message, did you, Doc?" Megan's words came out in a snarl." She held the gun inches from Quinn's face.

"You kept on seeing Thomas after I stopped therapy, and you worked at destroying his love for me. You told him to break up with me. You're no better than my Da or my Gram. You never cared about me at all! You just wanted to turn the one person who loved me against me with your lies! Now it's your turn to lose someone you care about."

"You're talking about Fiona, aren't you, Megan?" Quinn was trying to keep her voice calm. "She hasn't done anything to you; it's me you're angry with. Why don't you tell me where Fiona is?"

"Oh, I'll do more than tell you where she is. I'll show you. Come on, Doc, it's time for you and me to leave. We wouldn't want visitors spoiling the fun, would we?"

Megan shoved the gun hard into Quinn's ribs. "We'll take your car. Is that okay with you, Dr. Langston?" Megan asked sarcastically in the meek voice Quinn was accustomed to. She laughed and, again, became this new Megan that Quinn didn't know at all.

As they pulled out of the lane, Quinn saw Pike take flight from her study window. He stayed further back than usual, but she could still see him out of the corner of her eye as he followed the car. The sight of him gave her comfort.

They drove for a few miles before Megan said, "Turn here," and again shoved the gun hard into Quinn's ribs. Quinn felt anger rising in her, as it always did when confronted with a bully. Watching her father bully her mother while growing up left a lasting legacy. Now, she fought hard to maintain her calm demeanor.

They had turned down a little used lane. After about a mile, they came to an abandoned cottage surrounded by an overgrowth of shrubs and weeds. The tin roof of the structure was half gone, and the rest was severely rusted. It was evident that no one had used the cottage in years.

"Pull up close to the house and get out of the car." Megan walked around to Quinn's side of the car, motioning for her to climb out with the barrel of the gun. "Now, Dr. Langston, I'll show you what I've done with your friend."

Quinn had a sick feeling in the pit of her stomach as the two of them pushed through the thicket toward the cottage. As they approached the front door, Megan shoved her and motioned for her to go around to the side of the building. Quinn noticed a kind of trap door in the foundation of the old structure. Megan pushed Quinn to her knees and, still holding the gun, unlocked the thick door with her free hand. "See what good care I've taken of your friend?"

Quinn couldn't see anything in the dark crawl space for a few moments, but then, as her eyes adjusted, she made out the form of a woman, bound hand and foot, lying face up in the shallow space. At first, she was afraid that Fiona was dead, but then, she heard a low moan and saw her friend's face turn towards her. "Fiona!" There was no response.

Quinn turned towards Megan, "What have you done to her, you sick little bitch?"

Quinn felt the blow as Megan brought the gun down hard against her temple.

When Quinn opened her eyes again, she realized something was very wrong. She could barely move, and rocks were cutting into her back. Her head was throbbing. It took her a moment to regain her wits. Then, with a jolt, she realized that she, too, had been bound and was now lying in the cramped crawl space. The floor of the old building was less than a foot from her face. The floor joists on each side of her were even lower, so movement was almost impossible. Panic washed over her.

It felt like the floor of the cottage was pushing down on her. Then she saw Fiona lying nearby, on her side. She was making soft whimpering noises, like those of a frightened animal. As bad as this was for her, it was much worse for her friend, Quinn knew. Fiona had a terror of small spaces because of being locked inside a refrigerator as a child. Quinn pushed herself towards her. She could feel the sharp rocks tearing at her back with each slight movement. Ignoring the pain, she scooted closer. Finally, she could touch Fiona's arm with her bound hands. She would comfort her as best she could.

Quinn began to talk to Fiona, trying to pull her back from the darkest recesses of her mind. "Fiona, I'm going to get us out of here. I promise I'll get you out of here." There was no response apart from the continued whimpering. Quinn knew Fiona was breaking down, reverting to the most basic parts of her personality. Tears slid down Quinn's face. This was all her fault. If only she had seen Megan Murphy for what she was. Panic was, again, beginning to take her over.

Quinn tried to push the fear aside. Surely, she was forgetting something. What was it? Then she remembered Pike taking flight as they left the farm. Pike had followed her to this place. She knew he must still be somewhere close by.

Quinn tried to slow her breathing and get some air into her lungs. She pursed her lips to call to the bird. At first, she could not make a sound, but after a few more attempts, she gave one loud call. And then, another and another. She waited for what seemed an eternity, hoping Pike was near enough to hear.

Then Pike's call resounded back to her. Relief flooded Quinn. Pike would help them. He had to. He was the only thing that stood between them and certain death.

"Come on, Pike, find a way in. Help us." Quinn squeezed her eyes shut and began chanting the words over and over, like a mantra, "Come on, Pike; come on, Pike." It was the only thing keeping the terror from taking her over completely. "Come on, Pike."

Quinn was pretty sure she knew what Megan had planned. She would burn them alive by setting the house on fire, the way she had murdered her father. Before Megan had hit her with the gun, Quinn had noticed a can of petrol on the ground by the trap door. Now, Pike was their only hope. "Come on, Pike! Quinn closed her eyes again and tried to shut everything else out of her mind. Come on, Pike, help us!"

Just then, Quinn heard hard tapping as Pike used his powerful beak to chip away at the chinks in the stone foundation near where she and Fiona were lying. Suddenly, a tiny sliver of daylight appeared and then grew larger.

"Come on, Pike!" Quinn, again, squeezed her eyes shut, closing everything out but the steady tapping of Pike's beak on the stone.

Soon, Pike had made the hole large enough to hop through. Then he was next to her. She could see his sharp, intelligent eyes looking into hers. Tears of gratitude slid down her cheeks.

"The knots, Pike, undo the knots!" Quinn heard the desperate pleading in her voice.

Pike grabbed the rope with his beak and began working the knots. Quinn could feel the binding around her wrists loosening. Soon, Quinn was free. Pike worked on the ropes binding Fiona's ankles as Quinn loosened her hands. Fiona lay motionless, not responding to Quinn or trying to move.

"Come on, Fiona; we've got to get out of here."

Quinn could hear Megan's footsteps and a splashing sound above them. A wave of petrol fumes hit her as she scooted towards the opening Pike had made in the foundation. She pulled Fiona along with her as she moved. Once she reached the opening, Quinn kicked at the loosened stones, enlarging the hole as she did so. She could only hope Megan would not hear what she was doing. Quinn continued to whisper gentle words of encouragement to her friend as she worked. Fiona made no response.

Finally, the opening was large enough for Quinn to crawl through. Slowly, she pushed her way out, pulling Fiona out after her.

"And where do you think you two are going?" Megan stood near the opening Pike and Quinn had made in the foundation of the old building. She was pointing the gun at Quinn, and her face was contorted by the inner rage she now displayed with frightening clarity.

Quinn knew there was no use trying to appeal to this person, who was, in no way, the girl who had sat in her office, looking so cowed by life. This sociopathic creature felt nothing but a malicious desire to harm others. As Megan stepped towards her, Quinn frantically looked around her for a weapon.

Just then, Pike rose from the ground and flew straight at Megan. His sharp beak sank deeply into her cheek, drawing blood.

Megan screamed and stumbled forward towards Quinn, still holding the gun, but Pike was there again, and this time, his beak struck hard, catching Megan squarely in the eye.

Dropping the gun, Megan screamed, "My eye, my eye!" She wheeled around, holding one hand over her eye as she batted at Pike with the other. Pike repeatedly dove at her, mindful to keep just out of her reach.

Quinn suddenly spotted an old shovel leaning against the wall of a nearby shed. She ran to pick it up and quickly landed a hard blow to the side of Megan's head. Megan fell to the ground, moaning, unable to rise.

Quinn raised the shovel over Megan's head, poised to strike again. The anger she'd carried since childhood rose in her full force, but she stopped herself. She would not become the thing she hated.

Throwing the shovel aside, Quinn pulled Fiona up from where she had sunk against the wall and half-carried her towards the car. The keys were in the ignition. She struggled to get Fiona into the passenger seat, and then climbed into the car, pausing for just a moment to clear her head, which, she now realized, was pounding from the blow to her temple. Then, she quickly backed out of the lane and drove as fast as she could towards the village. She could see Pike flying next to them, staying close.

FIONA STARED at the ceiling in the examining room of the small medical clinic in Ballyfrannen, not responding to Quinn or the doctor examining her.

The young doctor turned to look at Quinn. "Except for a few scrapes and bruises, she appears to be fine physically. Mentally though, she is still in shock. It's probably best to take her home and make her comfortable. She'll come around once she is in her own environment. I gave her a sedative, so she'll sleep a lot for the rest of the day, and that will do her as much good as anything."

Suddenly, Quinn was overcome with exhaustion; she reached out to catch herself, fearing she was about to collapse. The doctor studied her briefly before gently taking her arm and leading her toward a chair, "You'd better have a seat and let me examine you, too."

"No, I'm fine. I need to sit down, that's all."

Dermot Brennan came into the room where Quinn was keeping watch over Fiona. He was not the same smug man he had been when Quinn and Fiona had visited him at the Garda station.

"We've already arrested Megan Murphy, Dr. Langston. She won't be bothering you or anyone else for a very long time; I can assure you of that." Dermot studiously avoided eye contact with Quinn as he spoke.

Suddenly, there was a commotion in the hallway. Quinn looked up to see the entire O'Callaghan family heading towards her; even Donal had come. His face was full of concern as he leaned heavily on his cane and hobbled down the hallway toward her and Fiona.

Quinn could feel her composure disintegrating at the sight of them.

They gathered around her as Margaret wrapped her in her arms, "You're alright now, Love. I've got you; you're alright now." Margaret gently rocked back and forth as she spoke.

Quinn felt whatever inner strength she had left give way. She heard herself sobbing as she buried her head in Margaret's shoulder.

Soon, they all left the clinic together, with Daniel gently leading Fiona out to Margaret's minivan.

Pike flew alongside as they headed towards the farm. Quinn cast grateful glances at the bird as they drove through the peaceful countryside, and he seemed still to be watchful and on guard.

As Quinn caught sight of her cottage in the distance, fresh tears streamed down her face. She realized how close she and Fiona had come to never seeing it again.

CHAPTER 26

Several weeks had passed since Quinn and Fiona's encounter with Megan Murphy. Quinn had resumed seeing her patients, and, little by little, life had began to take on a normal quality.

Megan Murphy was in jail, charged with the deaths of her father and grandmother, as well as that of Nola Baird. Megan had confessed to mistaking Nola for Quinn. She was also charged with the kidnapping and attempted murder of Fiona and Quinn.

Fiona was slowly recovering from her ordeal. Daniel had offered to stay at the cottage whenever Quinn was away. He would sit with Fiona in the kitchen, sipping tea and speaking in a quiet voice. Quinn could tell that Fiona found his presence comforting, but her face remained expressionless. She seldom spoke and was easily startled by even the slightest noise. Pike and Maggie also stayed close to Fiona, sensing her need for companionship.

Hattie had offered to care for the plants in Fiona's greenhouse. She said it was the least she could do. She still felt she had let her friends down by not discovering the truth about Megan Murphy. Fiona had not yet stepped outside the door of the cottage, but now Quinn felt it was time.

"Fiona, I'm going out to the greenhouse for a while, and I want you to come with me." Fiona allowed Quinn to take her by the hand and lead her through the sunny garden and into the little glass structure. For a few moments, they stood side by side, hand in hand, taking in the beauty of this quiet place. Quinn closed her eyes. She loved the smell of the moist soil and the fragrance of the flowers.

Fiona's breathing became less shallow. Slowly, she began taking deeper and deeper breaths until finally, she gave a large sigh of release. Quinn gently pulled her hand from Fiona's and started walking down the first aisle of plants, reaching out as she did toward one of the aged clay pots to place a delicate-looking seedling between her fingers.

"Don't touch my Bells of Ireland," bellowed Fiona. "And look at my Phlox and Zinnias! They've been over-watered." Fiona fussed with one plant and then another. "Bring me my gardening gloves, would you, Quinn? I'll be hours sorting this out."

Quinn did as she was told, smiling to herself, knowing her friend would find the healing she needed right here among the living things she loved most.

THOMAS LAFFERTY surprised Quinn a few weeks later by scheduling an appointment at the clinic. Even more surprising was how well dressed he was, and that he now wore his hair in a short, tousled style, and the light scent of soap and shampoo replaced the smell of tobacco.

Thomas apologized to Quinn for what Megan had done; he felt responsible for not seeing Megan for who she was. Quinn reminded him that even with her years of training, she hadn't seen Megan for who she was either. "Sometimes," Quinn said, "we only see what we want to see."

Thomas came regularly to the clinic after that and was making remarkable progress. He started taking classes at night and soon found a job as a computer programmer with a company in Cork City. He began dressing like a young professional, eating healthier, and working out regularly at a gym. At Quinn's suggestion, Thomas visited a dentist who placed porcelain veneers on his front teeth and cleaned and whitened the rest. The results were truly dramatic. Thomas no longer saw himself as worthless, and with that, he saw the worth of the people around him. He was not at all the same young man who had walked into Quinn's office all those months ago.

ONE DAY, as Quinn was feeding Tam and Hilda, she heard a car pull into the lane and turned to see Bruno Tricot walking towards her. She swore under her breath and wondered what he could possibly want. She had noticed work beginning on his property. Had he come to gloat?

"Hello, Dr. Langston. Would you mind if we spoke for a few moments?"

Bruno seemed very different from the man she remembered coming to her office. Still, she remained guarded. "What can I do for you, Mr. Tricot?" Quinn continued feeding the pigs as she spoke.

"I know you have no reason to want to talk to me after the way I have treated you, but I would very much like to tell you how sorry I am for how I have acted." Bruno paused for a moment. "You may have heard that my wife and I will soon be divorced, and I am no longer a rich man. I am not telling you these things to gain your sympathy. I am a much happier man than I have been in a very long time. I would like to think I am a wiser man, too." Bruno looked steadily into Quinn's eyes. "You and Fiona did not deserve to be treated in such a high-handed manner. There is no excuse for that kind of behavior." Bruno stared at the ground as he spoke.

Quinn felt herself softening towards this man. "I appreciate your apology, Mr. Tricot."

"Please call me Bruno; we are to be neighbors, after all," Bruno spoke humbly.

Quinn took a good look at Bruno. He had not only changed his demeanor, but he had also changed physically. Gone were the potbelly, stooped shoulders, and shuffling walk. He looked much younger and fitter than before.

Quinn smiled. "Alright, Bruno it is then." She stood petting Tam and Hilda for a moment. "I've been watching the progress of your house; any chance of getting a guided tour?"

Bruno brightened visibly, "Madame, nothing would please me more than to show you my modest new home."

Quinn walked through the partially completed structure as Bruno explained the floor plan. All the rooms looked out onto the sea.

The living room and kitchen were large rooms with many windows that took advantage of the view. An enormous stone fireplace stood at one end. A half-bath and laundry room on the north side of the house accommodated boots, coats, and all things needed for country life. The south side had a lovely glass conservatory, which provided magnificent views of both the sea and the rolling green hills. Upstairs were two nice-sized bedrooms, each with en suite bathrooms and, once again, beautiful views of the sea and surrounding countryside. The house had a wonderfully pleasant feel to it.

Quinn was pleased to finally be on good terms with her new neighbor. She actually looked forward to Bruno moving in. She was sure Fiona would enjoy helping Bruno fill the conservatory with plants of every description. Quinn wasn't sure if Hattie had met her new neighbor yet. She felt sure Hattie would eventually become friends with Bruno, too.

HATTIE MADE a habit of taking long walks. The tranquillity of the countryside seemed to soothe her soul. She still felt upset that she hadn't been more help to Quinn and Fiona. She had ruled Megan Murphy out completely. What was it about that girl that had fooled everyone?

Hattie tramped through the field that bordered the Tricots' property. It was a fine day; there wasn't a cloud in the sky, which rarely happens in Ireland. Wolfie trotted along at her side, easily keeping up with her long strides.

Still deep in thought, Hattie was surprised to see a man walking towards her. It must be Bruno Tricot, she thought. Hattie knew that Bruno's young wife had left him when she found out he'd lost all his money. Quinn had told her he was building a much smaller and simpler home on the large plot of land that Madeleine Tricot had been so obsessed with.

She might as well be neighborly and introduce herself, even though she was sure she wouldn't like him from all she'd heard.

Hattie put on her best fake smile and quickly picked up her pace to greet the famous Bruno Tricot. As she drew nearer, she began to have an odd sensation. Something about the way this man walked seemed vaguely familiar. How could that be?

"Hello, Madame, that's quite a large dog you've got there. An Irish wolfhound, isn't it? That is a breed that I, myself, am very fond of. Years ago, I gave a puppy of this breed to a very dear friend..." Bruno's voice trailed off, and then he recovered himself.

"Madame, I forget my manners; please allow me to introduce myself. I am Bruno Tricot. I believe you are the woman living in the cottage beside Fiona and Quinn. Am I right? Fiona has spoken of you. She said you had been a detective in England before moving here. That must have been an interesting profession."

Hattie felt jolted, as though lightning had struck her. It had been years since she had heard that voice, but she knew it just the same. It took her a moment to regain her senses.

"Bruno, my God, it's really you. After all these years, here you are, practically in my front garden."

Bruno Tricot stood staring at the tall, plain-faced older woman standing before him. Then, he, too, was struck by recognition.

"Antonia?" Bruno took a step backward. "Where have you come from? My wife—well, my soon-to-be former wife, told me you had come to our house and spoken with her. I couldn't believe it when she told me that. You don't know how badly I've wanted to find you through the years, to tell you how sorry I am for how I treated you."

"Really? You've been looking for me? That's odd because I've been looking for you, too." Hattie felt years of anger rising in her. Sensing her emotions, Wolfie began to growl softly.

Hattie laid a hand on the large dog's neck before continuing, "At least I did for many years after you left me on the eve of our wedding. Can you imagine how devastated I was? I gave up modeling and moved back to England. My life was never the same. Antonia disappeared that night, and I became Hattie Biggs again. Not glamorous or famous... or even loved." Hattie had said more than she'd meant to.

Bruno reached out to touch her arm, but Hattie jerked it away.

"Please, Antonia, you must allow me to explain. I never meant to hurt you. I thought I was doing the right thing by leaving. There was much you didn't know about Bruno Cabell. He was not the man you thought he was."

The hair stood up on Wolfie's neck, and his growl became more ominous.

Bruno stepped back, "Your dog, he does not seem to like me very much."

"He's a good judge of character." Hattie couldn't believe the situation she now found herself in. The only man she had ever loved, the man she had been searching for since that night so many years ago, would now be her next-door neighbor. She had imagined many scenarios of meeting Bruno again, but never anything so mundane as this.

"Antonia, please, at least hear me out. Is there somewhere we can go to talk?"

After all the years of wondering, Hattie had to admit she wanted to hear what Bruno had to say. "I suppose we could go inside my cottage to talk more comfortably." Hattie turned and walked toward her little stone cottage with Wolfie at her heels.

Bruno looked incredulous. "Antonia, of all the places in the world either of us could have lived; how could we have ended up next door to one another? How strange life is."

"Please stop calling me Antonia; no one calls me that anymore." Hattie couldn't remember the last time she had felt so flustered.

Wolfie, now comfortable with the situation, trotted a little way off to follow a rabbit's scent.

Suddenly, a smile began to play at the corners of Hattie's mouth. She clamped her teeth firmly together in an effort to put an end to such foolishness, but her steps felt lighter as they walked the short distance and entered the cottage together.

*a*gnes Meek sat in Quinn's office, waiting for her session to begin. She had lost a great deal of weight, and she no longer fidgeted with her handbag or widened her eyes to stare blankly at Quinn when asked a question. Agnes was now a more self-assured and confident woman.

"Aren't you going to ask me what my week was like?" Agnes seemed almost bursting with excitement.

"Alright, Agnes, what was your week like?" Quinn asked as she laughed.

"Well, you knew I used to work in a pub before I won the lottery, didn't you?" Agnes didn't wait for Quinn to answer. "Anyway, I had a best friend back then. Her name was Josie, and, well, don't hold this against her, but she is Megan Murphy's mother. Can you believe it? We hadn't spoken in years. I think it was my fault, really. After winning that money, I began to suspect that anyone who was nice to me was only out to get some of it. "

"I'm getting way off track, though. What I'm trying to tell you is that after the police arrested Megan , I stopped by to see Josie. She was in a terrible state. You can imagine how devastating it has been for her to find out her daughter is a murderer. She couldn't work, and her bills were piling up. I really felt sorry for her, and then I realized I was in a position to help, so I wrote her a nice big check. She was so grateful; she cried and hugged me for the longest time."

"The odd thing is that it made me so happy to help Josie. Honestly, Dr. Langston, I don't think winning that money has brought me much happiness until now, but I'm getting off track again."

Agnes' laughter filled the tiny office. "I met Josie's son too. He's a good kid, nothing like his sister. Anyway, we've become best friends over the last few weeks. Josie says she doesn't know what she would have done if I hadn't helped her." Agnes beamed with pride.

"Dr. Langston, I've asked Josie and her son to move in with me. I've got such a large house, and it's been just me rattling around in it for so long. Do you think that's crazy?"

"No, Agnes, that isn't crazy at all. In fact, I've never been prouder of you than I am right now."

JOZEF ABRAM SAT SLUMPED on a bar stool in one of Ballyfrannen's seedier pubs. He was on his fourth Tetra, a strong Polish beer. He usually preferred Guinness, but this beer reminded him of home.

Yesterday, he fought with the foreman at the construction site and had been let go. Two days before that, his wife had left for Poland. Her mother had arranged airfare for her and the children.

He was supposed to see Dr. Langston for his weekly appointment today, but he didn't plan on ever going back. "To hell with all of them," he mumbled under his breath in Polish, quickly draining the glass of Tetra and ordering another pint of the strong beer.

Fiona was doing much better. So much better, Quinn had decided to have a dinner party, something she would never have dreamed of doing back in the States. She was so grateful for her new life here in Ireland, and she knew Fiona was too. What better way to express her gratitude than to have everyone she cared about sitting at her table?

Quinn, Fiona, Margaret, and Hattie sat planning the guest list for the party. So far, they had the four of them, plus Daniel, Maureen, and Donal. They were also inviting Cathal Fagan and his wife and Owen Gilpatrick.

Owen now lived with his niece in town. He had visited the farm many times and was delighted with the changes Quinn and Fiona had made.

Quinn wanted to invite Agnes Meek, even though she was a patient. Agnes had changed so much since she had first entered Quinn's office. Quinn now felt a genuine friendship towards her. Since she was inviting Agnes, she might as well ask Thomas, too. She felt so much pride in how Thomas had turned his life around.

An argument, of sorts, had broken out at the idea of inviting Bruno Tricot. Hattie was firmly against it. Her meeting with Bruno had given her some closure, at least. But Hattie wasn't sure she would ever forgive him. Wasn't it bad enough that he was to be her next-door neighbor without having to sit down to dinner with him?

Fiona, who was fond of Bruno because of his love of gardening, was just as firmly for it. Quinn and Margaret were both tired of all the quarreling.

"Okay," said Quinn, "let's flip a coin. Heads we invite him, and tails we don't."

Margaret reached into her pocket and pulled out a coin. She looked sternly at Fiona and Hattie before flipping it into the air over the kitchen table. It landed heads.

Fiona stuck her tongue out at Hattie.

"Alright, Fiona, could you try to act like an adult just this once?" Quinn couldn't keep the laughter out of her voice. It was so lovely to have the old Fiona back.

"Oh, alright, I guess I can sit at the other end of the table and ignore him." Hattie didn't seem as upset as she might have been.

None of the women failed to notice the way Hattie kept suppressing a smile, though. She seemed to smile a lot lately.

The next sticking point was Colin Brodie. Again, Fiona was for it, but it was Quinn who was against the idea this time.

"Fiona, you know I'll be so uncomfortable if Colin is here. We have hardly spoken in such a long time. I'm sure he wouldn't even be interested in coming to our little dinner party."

"Well, that shows what you know, Quinnie. I've already spoken to Colin; he would love to come!"

"Fiona, you didn't! I can't believe you would invite him without asking me first!"

Ignoring Quinn, Fiona grabbed a muffin from the plate of freshly baked treats Margaret had brought and took a large bite.

Margaret laughed, "What a bunch of eejits I've got for friends," but her voice held only affection. "Now, are we going to plan the food for this party or not?"

THE DAY of the party arrived, and Quinn was a bundle of nerves. She couldn't remember the last time she had hosted a dinner party—certainly not since her divorce from Jack.

She and Fiona had been busy for a week making sure the cottage was in order. Everything had been dusted, polished, and scrubbed. Margaret had helped with the menu and the cooking. She wouldn't have it any other way. She reminded them that all her years of running a bed & breakfast had taught her how to cook for a large gathering, and anyway, she said, she was a far better cook than they were.

Finally, the guests were seated around the large pine table Quinn had brought from the States. Everything looked lovely. Margaret's best china, silver, and Waterford goblets looked elegant on the antique tablecloth Margaret had also loaned them for the occasion. The candles, set in silver candlesticks atop the table, gave the room a wonderful glow, and the food looked delicious. People were chatting amiably with one another. Agnes Meek was having a lively conversation with Owen Gilpatrick, who seemed flattered by the attention. Thomas Lafferty had asked if he could bring a date, and he and a rather pleasant-looking girl were now having a quiet conversation with Cathal Fagan and his wife. Bruno was seated next to Margaret and her parents, and he seemed comfortable enough listening to Donal tell one of his many colorful stories. The only person who had not yet arrived was Hattie. Quinn wondered if seeing Bruno again was proving too much for her.

Just as Quinn tried to get Fiona's attention to ask if she had spoken to Hattie, a tall, elegantly dressed woman entered the room. She wore a well-cut, black dress with a fitted waist that flattered her slender figure. Blonde hair fell in soft curls around her face as she moved. Her makeup was expertly done and drew attention to her finely sculpted features. Her eyes were luminous, and she was genuinely stunning when she smiled.

There was a collective gasp from the guests seated at the table. No one looking at this woman would be surprised to learn that she had once been one of the top models in the world.

Quinn finally found her voice, "Hattie, is that you?"

Hattie laughed, "Oh, it's me, alright, Quinn. I just fixed myself up a little."

Hattie seated herself directly across the table from Bruno Tricot. Quinn looked in Bruno's direction for the first time since Hattie's arrival. He seemed almost frozen as he sat staring across the table at Hattie.

The room was so quiet you could hear a pin drop. All eyes were now on Hattie and Bruno.

"Antonia, ... my dear, sweet Antonia." The words were said with great tenderness as Bruno continued to stare at Hattie. Then he looked down at his lap, trying to regain his composure. "I'm sorry, I mean, Hattie." Bruno cleared his throat and dabbed at his forehead with his napkin before continuing. "It is so good to see you again. I, ah... please forgive me; I seem to be at a loss for words."

Hattie took a sip of wine, and then slowly set her glass back down on the table. She looked around the room and smiled. "Would you all please stop staring at me like I just stepped off a spaceship?"

At that, everyone laughed, and the tension seemed to dissolve from the room. People began to chat with one another again as dishes were passed around the table. Even Quinn felt relaxed and finally able to enjoy herself. Fiona had handled the seating arrangement, and Quinn was secretly pleased to be seated next to Colin Brodie. Their arms brushed as they both reached for their wine glasses. Quinn felt a tingling sensation go up her spine.

"Is everything alright at your end of the table?" Fiona seemed to have a twinkle in her eye as she waited for Quinn's response.

"Just don't start River Dancing or anything, okay, Fee?"

Fiona laughed by way of a response.

Each person seated at the table had played a role in Quinn's life since she and Fiona had moved to this place. A profound feeling of gratitude swept over her. There was nowhere on earth she would rather be than here in Ireland. The air stirred slightly. Quinn knew there was something more. Something she didn't know yet. She also knew she would embrace it, whatever it was, because it had led her here. She caught Fiona's eye and saw that her friend's emotions mirrored her own.

Fiona raised her glass in Quinn's direction. "To Ireland, Quinn."

Quinn responded by raising her glass, "To Ireland, Fee." The two women smiled at each other; years of friendship made more words unnecessary.